W9-ABW-409

Violet's Defiant Daughter

Violet's Defiant Daughter

BOOK SEVEN

of the
*A Life of Faith:
Violet Travilla*
Series

Based on the characters by
Martha Finley

MCP
Mission City Press

Book Seven of the *A Life of Faith: Violet Travilla* Series

Violet's Defiant Daughter
Copyright © 2006, Mission City Press, Inc. All Rights Reserved.

Published by Mission City Press, Inc.

This book is based on the *Elsie Dinsmore* series written by Martha Finley and first published in 1868 by Dodd, Mead & Company.

Cover & Interior Design: Richmond & Williams
Cover Photography: Michelle Grisco Photography
Typesetting: BookSetters

Unless otherwise indicated, all Scripture references are from the Holy Bible, New International Version (NIV). Copyright © 1973, 1978, 1984 by International Bible Society. Used by permission of Zondervan Publishing House, Grand Rapids, MI. All rights reserved.

For more information, write to Mission City Press at 202 Second Avenue South, Franklin, Tennessee 37064, or visit our Web Site at:

www.alifeoffaith.com

Library of Congress Catalog Card Number: 2005924797
Finley, Martha
        Violet's Defiant Daughter
        Book Seven of the *A Life of Faith: Violet Travilla* Series
        ISBN: 1-928749-23-2

Printed in the United States of America
1 2 3 4 5 6 7 8 — 10 09 08 07 06

— FOREWORD —

*L*ittle did Violet Travilla anticipate how a tall professor of Greek and Latin would change her life. But having given her heart to him in *Violet's Bumpy Ride*, the previous volume in the *A Life of Faith: Violet Travilla* series, Vi must now win the hearts of the professor's three children. Lessons in the meaning of love, trust, and faith will be learned, yet one young girl's determination to drive Violet away may prove more than Vi can handle.

Violet's Defiant Daughter is the seventh novel in the series based on fictional characters created by Miss Martha Finley — the author of the Elsie Dinsmore books published in the nineteenth and early twentieth centuries. Miss Finley's commitment to helping young people follow the Lord's path as they faced the challenges of their bygone era brought millions of readers to her books. And her message of faith and hope is kept alive in the Violet Travilla series. The stories are new, but the principles for godly living are timeless, and Mission City Press is honored to continue forward in Miss Finley's noble footsteps.

∾ VICTORIAN AMUSEMENTS ∾

In the latter half of the nineteenth century, after the Civil War, many Americans began to enjoy something that few had ever experienced before — leisure. With time to spare from their daily labors, upper- and middle-class Americans in the Victorian Age looked for new ways to entertain and amuse themselves. It was an era of great

v

inventions, and many practical innovations, like the light-bulb and the automobile, also provided more opportunities for entertainment. Other inventions—including the phonograph, the handheld camera, and the Kinetoscope followed by projected "living pictures" (movies)—literally changed the way Americans understood the world.

Railroads, steamships, and the automobile opened up new avenues for travel, and Americans, particularly those who lived in cities, began to plan vacations to places near and far. Most working people had no more than a week or two each year for holidays. But for the wealthy, long summer stays at the country's growing number of expensive resort hotels (like the Grand Hotel on Mackinac Island in Michigan, which included an 880-foot veranda with views of two of the Great Lakes) and health spas or months of travel in Europe were in order. The rich also constructed retreats for themselves. These were grand establishments, probably best seen today in Newport, Rhode Island, where the Vanderbilts, the Astors, and others of America's new multi-millionaires built palatial "summer cottages" with ocean views.

The Victorians took great interest in the beauty and the science of the natural world. Middle-class vacationers might journey to the mountains for camping and communing with nature, or choose seaside or lake retreats for fishing, boating, and swimming. Places of great natural splendor, especially Niagara Falls, had become popular with tourists early in the century, but without regulation, Niagara was soon cluttered with businesses catering to the tourist trade and other forms of development. What was called "The Shame of Niagara" prompted a new movement to preserve and manage the country's natural wonders for the benefit of all. The struggle between preservation and industrial/commercial development went on for decades. In 1864, President Abraham Lincoln signed Congressional legislation protecting the Yosemite Valley in California "for public use, resort, and recreation. . . inalienable for all time." The U.S. did not have a true national park system until 1916.

The first city parks, like New York's Central Park and Philadelphia's Fairmount Park, were designed as idealized natural settings where harried city dwellers could escape their daily lives with leisurely strolls or carriage rides through nature. But in the latter part of the century, a new kind of park began to appear in many cities and towns — "playground parks" with services oriented to their local neighborhoods. In addition to swings, slides, and sandboxes for children, these parks often included athletic fields, a field house and/or gymnasium which also was used as a community club, and later, swimming pools. Electric lighting made it possible to enjoy these community parks in the evening.

Another kind of park was very popular with people of all economic classes: the commercial amusement park where, for a relatively small cost, people could enjoy thrilling rides (roller coasters and Ferris wheels were standard by 1900), carnival-type games, fun houses, and sideshows. The most famous of the amusement parks was Coney Island in Brooklyn, New York, which prospered in spite of two major fires in the 1890s.

For many Americans, however, the idea of just having a good time seemed strange, and people worried that pure entertainment was decadent and could lead to laziness and a general moral decline. So the notion of using leisure time for education and self-improvement became popular. Many

of today's great museums, libraries, and zoos were funded by people of wealth as a means of bringing culture into the free time of the masses. Beginning in 1886, for example, industrialist Andrew Carnegie donated almost $40 million to finance the construction of 1,679 public libraries in cities and towns across the U.S.

The Chautauqua movement, started in 1878 by John Vincent, began as an enterprise to encourage "reading and study in nature, art, science and sacred literature, in conjunction with the routine of daily life . . . ." Chautauqua (named for its birthplace in New York) was a kind of home-based, group reading and study course. Chautauqua's four-year program promised the equivalent of a college-level education. Participants could also attend summer sessions at the Lake Chautauqua headquarters in the rustic Allegheny Mountains.

The Chautauqua concept inspired imitators across the country. Summer communities that combined intellectual, cultural, and religious learning flourished, as did Christian "campgrounds" that focused more on religious study and activities. These communities were usually owned by an association and consisted of large tracts of land, divided into house lots that were leased to members for ninety-nine years. Other amenities might include a hotel and boarding-house for guests of summer residents, a communal dining hall, a gymnasium, athletic fields and maybe tennis courts and a swimming pool, and a church or chapel for daily worship services and lectures by visiting ministers, scholars, and guest speakers.

It was finally being understood that women needed healthy, vigorous exercise as much as men. Calisthenics, a set of exercises developed to promote physical health and

grace, was introduced in schools and gymnasiums as the female equivalent of the more demanding gymnastic exercise of men. Women and girls didn't play baseball or football like their brothers, but they could enjoy skating. Ice skating was a winter activity, but roller skating could be enjoyed year-round, and indoor rinks did booming business in the 1870s. The Casino in New York City was so large that a thousand people could skate its wood-floored rink while another thousand watched from the balcony level.

The "high wheeler" bicycle was introduced in the 1870s, but its cumbersome design—large front wheel and small rear wheel or wheels—made it very difficult to ride, and impossible for women in their long skirts and petticoats. The first "safety" bike, with two wheels of the same size and a lighter frame, started the cycling craze in 1884. But women were still excluded from the fun because the bike had a stabilizing crossbar that made it difficult for women to manage their skirts with modesty. The Victor, with no crossbar and enclosed gears, opened the sport of bike riding to females when it was introduced in 1887. Biking was a serious alternative to travel on crowded trains and in horse-drawn carriages and gave people the means to get away from their cities and towns for a day or two and enjoy the countryside. Bicycle clubs, which organized biking excursions and included members of both sexes, were all the rage at the end of the century. As women were included in more physical activities—biking, hiking, camping, and swimming—their clothing also changed. Skirts were shorter and cut for ease of movement. Bathing suits began to evolve to allow actual swimming. And "daring" females, with the approval of many physicians, abandoned their laced corsets in favor of more comfortable undergarments.

Violet's Defiant Daughter

Not everyone had much leisure, however; the poor and working classes, including farmers, spent most of their waking hours earning enough to feed and house their families. They didn't get many days off, much less lengthy vacations. But they found ways to have fun. Children from poor and working-class families were creative at making their own entertainment. A rusty tin can could start an intense game of kick-the-can (a lot like soccer when played by a group). A piece of clothesline was all that was needed for skipping rope. Catch could be played with a ball made of cloth scraps, and a rock or stick could be used to scratch hopscotch squares on the ground. Marbles could be played with smooth, rounded pebbles and even round nuts. Dolls made of rags or dried corn husks inspired young imaginations just as well as the costly china dolls bought by people of means.

Entertainment opportunities for the working class expanded as the century neared its end. Vaudeville (variety) theaters featured music, dancing, and comedy acts for audiences of low-income families. Moving pictures projected on screens were added to the vaudeville programs in the 1890s, and independent storefront movie houses—later called "nickelodeons" because the entrance fee was five cents—were open in New York and New Orleans as early as 1896. A decade later, there were an estimated 5,000 nickelodeons across the nation. Professional and collegiate sports—especially baseball and football—drew people of all classes. Ladies did *not* attend what was probably the most popular spectator sport of the age—boxing, or prizefighting.

Well before movies arrived, rich and poor alike could attend musical shows, Wild West shows, circuses, and other performing acts that traveled the country. "Opera

houses" were built even in small towns for visiting theater, opera, and dance companies as well as local events of importance, such as a high school graduation. In most rural communities and small towns, homegrown public entertainments usually included holiday celebrations (the most popular was the annual Fourth of July picnic); county and state fairs with their agricultural exhibits and sideshow attractions; church socials, dances, and gatherings hosted by the growing number of clubs and fraternal lodges; football and baseball competitions between local amateur or college teams; and political meetings.

Fun at Home: Middle-class Americans didn't have to go far for amusement. With their growing incomes, they began to spend some of their money on what we would call home entertainment. There was a great craze for parlor organs and pianolas (mechanical pianos) as well as real pianos. The phonograph—a machine that recorded sound on a rotating metal cylinder—was patented by Thomas Edison in 1877 and underwent a number of improvements in the 1880s and 1890s. The public was introduced to recorded sound by coin-operated machines (the origin of jukeboxes) in amusement parks, drug stores, and elsewhere. With Emile Berliner's invention of a process for duplicating a recording on round "plates" (records), Americans could buy phonograph machines and play records in their own homes. Though early recordings included speeches, dramatic readings, and even animal and mechanic sounds, it was music that Americans preferred.

The Victorians also loved to compete, and favorite yard games included croquet, lawn tennis, shuttlecocks (badminton), and archery—all thought to be tame enough for women and girls to play. Children's outdoor games were much the same as today: hide-and-seek (also called I Spy!), Whoop (during which only one person hides), Puss, Puss in the Corner (similar to modern musical chairs), various forms of tag and Follow the Leader, marbles, jump rope, spinning tops, jacks, and hopscotch. Boys often played "rounders," which is similar to baseball, though baseball had become the favorite by the end of the century.

Card games including Whist, Bridge, Euchre, and Five Hundred were popular with adults. Children's card games tended to be instructive, like games with Bible story themes and *Authors*, a game that promoted learning about the most famous writers of the time. There were just-for-fun card games too, including the still popular *Old Maid*. The earliest American board games, like *The Mansion of Happiness*, introduced in 1843, and *The Checkered Game of Life* (1860), encouraged moral behavior and good deeds. Religious board games, like the later *Going to Jerusalem*, were considered suitable for play on the Sabbath.

With improvements in color printing and packaging, the number and variety of board games quickly increased. Many of these games, like *Bulls and Bears: The Great Wall Street Game* (1883), emphasized the dream of achieving great wealth, and others centered on specific businesses and occupations (*The Game of Store, Corner Grocery, The Game of Messenger Boy or Merit Rewarded*). A very popular travel game, first sold in 1890, was *Round the World with Nellie Bly*, based on the true-life adventure of newspaper-woman Elizabeth Jane Cochran, who wrote under the pen name of Nellie Bly. In 1889, Bly thrilled readers with her daily reports of circling the globe in seventy-two days—a feat that bested the fictional record of Phileas Fogg, hero

Foreword

of French author Jules Verne's novel *Around the World in Eighty Days*.

Other tabletop games enjoyed by adults and children were checkers (also known as *draughts*), dominoes, chess, Carrom Board (a game played by pushing disks into the corners of a polished wooden board), and jackstraws (today's pick-up-sticks). Jigsaw puzzles intrigued people of all ages. Victorian families and their friends also loved parlor games like charades, riddles, conundrums ("Why is the letter D like a sailor?" "They both follow the C."), and other word puzzles. Some parlor games required physical agility. For instance, to play Blowing the Feather, participants sat in a circle and held a sheet at chin level. A feather placed on the sheet had to be blown in different directions so that it could not be grabbed by a single player outside the circle. Such games allowed young men and women to interact within the bounds of proper conduct.

The spread of public education greatly increased the demand for inexpensive and entertaining books, magazines, newspapers, and other reading materials. Literature specifically for children and young people was introduced into the United States from England in the early nineteenth century. Until then, most young readers were limited to school texts and whatever publications their parents acquired for themselves. In 1824, the first monthly magazine for children, the *Juvenile Miscellany*, was published by Lydia Maria Child—an ardent abolitionist, champion of Native American causes, and the often uncredited author of the nation's favorite Thanksgiving poem, "Over the River and Through the Woods." The success of Mrs. Child's magazine inspired a new branch of American publishing and prompted public libraries to establish specialized children's collections.

Violet's Defiant Daughter

Series books were very popular. Horatio Alger, who wrote more than a hundred books on the theme of poor but honest boys who achieve great success, sold more than twenty million copies. Series like the stories of Frank Merriwell by William G. Patten (published in magazines and as books) and Martha Finley's Elsie Dinsmore books were grabbed up by young readers eager for the latest tales of their favorite hero or heroine. These stories often included strong moral, ethical, and inspirational lessons in the fictional context of thrilling adventures and dramatic conflicts.

Many of the early books for children and teens, however, were not very exciting or well written and are barely remembered today. But by the second half of the nineteenth century, talented American and British authors including Louisa May Alcott (*Little Women*, *Little Men*), Mark Twain (*The Adventures of Tom Sawyer* and *Huckleberry Finn*), Robert Louis Stevenson (*Treasure Island*, *A Child's Garden of Verses*), Lewis Carroll (*Alice's Adventures in Wonderland*) were writing fine stories and poetry that emphasized adventure and fantasy. Translations of books like *Swiss Family Robinson* by J. D. Wyss and the fairy tales of Hans Christian Andersen added to the growing body of classic literature for children and young people.

At home, on vacation, and at public events, Americans of the late nineteenth century were learning to use their new leisure time—for pleasure, for instruction, and, as it was often said in those days, for the betterment of their minds, bodies, and spirits.

TRAVILLA/DINSMORE FAMILY TREE

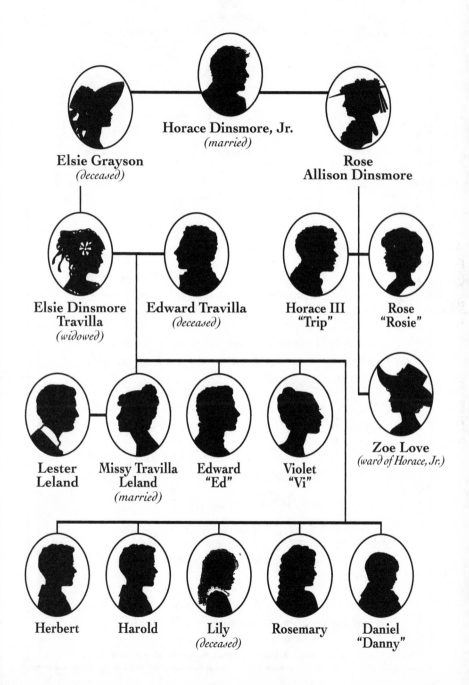

Elsie Grayson
(deceased)

Horace Dinsmore, Jr.
(married)

Rose
Allison Dinsmore

Elsie Dinsmore
Travilla
(widowed)

Edward Travilla
(deceased)

Horace III
"Trip"

Rose
"Rosie"

Lester
Leland

Missy Travilla
Leland
(married)

Edward
"Ed"

Violet
"Vi"

Zoe Love
(ward of Horace, Jr.)

Herbert

Harold

Lily
(deceased)

Rosemary

Daniel
"Danny"

Setting

*T*he story is set in the summer of 1884 in India Bay, the Southern seaport city where Vi Travilla's mission, Samaritan House, is located in the district of Wildwood.

Characters

Violet Travilla (Vi) — age 21, the third child of Elsie and the late Edward Travilla.

Elsie Dinsmore Travilla — a wealthy widow, owner of Ion Plantation; mother of Vi and her six brothers and sisters:

> **Elsie Travilla Leland (Missy)** — almost 27; lives in Rome with her husband, **Lester**, and their young son.

> **Edward Travilla, Jr. (Ed)** — age 25; manager of Ion.

> **Herbert** and **Harold Travilla** — twins, age 18; students at a great Eastern university.

> **Rosemary Travilla** — age 14.

> **Daniel Travilla (Danny)** — age 10.

Ben and **Crystal Johnson** — longtime household servants at Ion.

Horace Dinsmore, Jr. and his wife, **Rose** — Vi's grandparents and owners of The Oaks Plantation.

Zoe Love — age 19, daughter of a deceased American diplomat and ward of Horace Dinsmore, Jr.

∞ SAMARITAN HOUSE ∞

Mrs. Maurene O'Flaherty — widow of a famous composer; Vi's companion and friend.

Enoch and **Christine Reeve** — caretaker and housekeeper at Samaritan House, and their young son, **Jacob.**

Mrs. Mary Appleton — Samaritan House's cook, and her daughter, **Polly**, age 6.

Miss Emily Clayton — a nurse.

Dr. David Bowman — a physician.

Miss Alma Hansen — a young seamstress from Germany, whose older brother, **Rudy**, is in California.

∞ OTHERS ∞

Mark Raymond — a college professor and archaeologist; a widowed father, recently moved to India Bay with his three children:

> **Max** — age 12
>
> **Lucilla (Lulu)** — age 10
>
> **Grace (Gracie)** — age 6

Miss Bessie Moran — the Raymonds' housekeeper; **Kaki Kennon**, the Raymonds' housemaid; and **Elwood Hogg**, the Raymonds' gardener and driver.

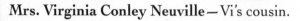

Mrs. Virginia Conley Neuville — Vi's cousin.

Mrs. Kidd and the members of an India Bay women's club — volunteers at the mission.

Miss Penelope Pepper — daughter of India Bay's richest family.

Ralph — the Pepper family's footman.

Reverend and **Mrs. Stephens**, **Widow Amos**, **Megan Mooney**, **Tilda Nedley**, **Mr. Hogg**, the butcher, his sons **Lynwood** and **Dagwood**, and others — residents of Wildwood.

Mr. Archibald — a master carpenter.

Dr. and **Mrs. Silas Lansing** — prominent supporters of Vi's mission.

Miss Susan Broadbent — founder of the Female Academy in India Bay.

Mr. Thomas Gibbons — owner of Coastal Telephonic Communications, Inc.

Mr. and **Mrs. Melanzana**, **Mr. Hedgegrow**, and others — members of the Melanzana Circus.

Tobias Clinch — owner of the Wildwood Hotel and Saloon.

Mr. and **Mrs. Embery**, **Mary Lacey**, and others — members of the Dinsmore family.

CHAPTER

1

Good-bye
for a While

*Go in peace. Your journey
has the LORD'S
approval.*

JUDGES 18:6

Good-bye for a While

*I*t was a perfect summer morning to everyone except Violet Travilla. She'd awakened at dawn. A gentle, cool breeze ruffled the lace curtains at her bedroom window, but she didn't feel its soft touch. As the sun rose, birds began to sing, but Vi didn't hear their cheerful chirps and twitters. She washed and dressed without interest in what she was doing. She was more careless than usual as she pinned her thick dark hair into a simple chignon, and several untidy strands spilled from the twist of hair at the back of her head.

She took her Bible from her bedside table, slumped into her rocking chair, and opened the small black book to a place marked with a bit of ribbon. She tried to concentrate her thoughts, but she didn't even realize that she was reading the same passage she had read the night before. Nothing that morning seemed to penetrate her consciousness. She closed the Bible on her lap, leaned back in her chair, shut her eyes, and began to speak with her Heavenly Friend.

"How can I feel this way, when others are suffering real loss and sorrow?" she said in a weary tone. "Mark will be gone for only six weeks, yet I feel as if I might never see him again. He tells me there is no need to worry. But Yucatan — it is so far away, so remote. Who knows what dangers await him there?"

She stopped speaking and bit her bottom lip. "Oh, please forgive me, dear Lord," she said after a few moments. "It's not for me to know what lies ahead for any of us. I trust You with all my heart to guide my path and

Mark's. I trust that whatever awaits us, You will hold us in Your hands and guide our steps. I believe in Your promise, that You will give us no more than we can bear."

She paused again, listening closely to the voice in her heart, and a sweet smile slowly came to her lips. "I begin to understand," she said. "My fears for Mark's safety are part of my love for him. Yet with You in our hearts, our love for one another is so much stronger than fear. You have given me the answer, Lord. It is right here, under my hands, in Your Holy Word. 'There is no fear in love. But perfect love drives out fear, because fear has to do with punishment. The one who fears is not made perfect in love.'

"With Your love, I can drive out my fears. You are always here for me, to hear my worries and to remind me to trust in You without hesitation. You are my perfect Friend, and whenever I feel this weight of fear, You will lift it from me, as You lift it from me now."

Vi clutched her well-worn Bible tightly in her hands and said in a clear voice, "Dear Lord, please bless Mark on his journey and watch over him with Your love that drives out fear. For myself, I ask that You strengthen me that I may resist my fears and be strong for Mark and for his children while he is away. Help me to help them."

Vi sat forward in her chair and finished her prayer by asking her Heavenly Father to grant His blessings on all her family and friends. When she opened her eyes, the morning sun that filled her room was so bright that she blinked several times before she could focus. She felt like someone who had been inside a deep tunnel. Yet in the darkness, God's gentle hand had taken her hand, and He had led her into the light. Her feelings of anxiety and weariness had vanished.

Good-bye for a While

She stood up and said, "Thank You, Lord, for Your endless patience with me. And thank You for this beautiful day! It is a wonderful day for my beloved to begin his adventure."

Vi made a point to tidy her hair before she hurried downstairs. In the kitchen of the mission named Samaritan House, she found her friends already at their tasks. Mrs. O'Flaherty was beating eggs in a bowl while Mary Appleton, the mission's cook, was turning thick slices of bacon in a large iron skillet. Christine Reeve, the housekeeper, was sitting at the kitchen table, holding her giggling, squirming toddler on her lap and trying to feed him his oatmeal porridge.

Mrs. O'Flaherty, Vi's wise friend, confidante, and companion in the management of Samaritan House—which served the poor people of the Wildwood district in the seaport city of India Bay—said, "You were a little late in rising today, Vi."

"Not in rising," Vi replied with a smile. "I was slow in getting started and needed help from our Lord to get myself out of a mood."

Mrs. O'Flaherty smiled knowingly, for she had correctly guessed the reason for Vi's tardiness. Professor Mark Raymond was leaving in just a few hours for an archaeological trip in Mexico, and he would be gone for at least six weeks.

"Well, Alma has already departed," Mrs. O'Flaherty said, as she turned her attention to some fresh corn muffins that required buttering. "Enoch had the buggy ready practically at the crack of dawn. He wants to get back by lunchtime, so he can help the carpenters at the shelter this afternoon."

Violet's Defiant Daughter

Vi looked around her and experienced the pleasant feeling of warmth that comes from being among friends. As she set plates on the rough kitchen table, she thought about Alma Hansen, the young German immigrant who had been living at the mission since the previous winter. Alma was going to Ion, Vi's family estate in the countryside, to stay for almost a week. Alma would be stitching and sewing for friends of Vi's mother, ladies who were delighted to find a dressmaker to create fashionable gowns for themselves and their daughters.

Mrs. O'Flaherty interrupted Vi's thoughts, saying, "It is a day for departures."

"I was thinking that earlier," Vi said, "but I have decided it is really a day for beginnings."

Mrs. O smiled at her young friend and said, "That's the right attitude, Vi girl. Will Professor Raymond be stopping by before he leaves?"

"Just after breakfast," Vi replied, her smile broadening.

"And will you go to the railway station to see him off?" Mary asked.

"No," Vi said. "That honor will belong to Max and Lulu and Gracie. This is their first separation from their father in many months — since he reunited their family. Bidding him farewell should be their time together."

"Quite wise of you," Mrs. O'Flaherty said.

Now the adults at Samaritan House were aware that Vi and Professor Mark Raymond were engaged to be married. But because the engagement had not been officially announced and everyone understood that the circumstances were complicated, they had agreed among themselves not to speak of Vi and Mark's future plans. They also knew how important the next six weeks were. In Mark's absence, Vi would be spending much of her time with his children, getting to know them better and building trust and love, so the children would welcome her into their family. Of course, none of Vi's friends doubted that Vi would easily win the hearts of the three Raymond children.

Counting the plates on the table, Vi realized that someone was not present. "Where's Polly?" she asked, referring to Mary's six-year-old daughter.

"In your office, feeding Jam," Mary said. "I declare, Polly treats that orange cat like the Queen of Sheba. I had to chop up the best leftovers from last night's fish for Jam's breakfast. Polly insisted."

Vi laughed, "I do believe our Jam thinks she is the queen of cats, if not of Sheba."

A few moments later, Polly skipped happily into the kitchen. A quiet child by nature, she no longer displayed any shyness with the residents of the mission. Everyone took their seats, while near his mother's feet, little Jacob busily stacked wooden blocks. Mrs. O'Flaherty said grace, including a special request for God's blessing on Professor Raymond and his children.

The women were washing their breakfast dishes when there was a tapping at the kitchen door. A tall, sandy-haired man with a thick mustache entered. Despite her determination to be strong, at the sight of him, Vi nearly dropped the china sugar bowl she was holding.

It was still early. Dr. David Bowman and Miss Emily Clayton, the mission's physician and nurse, had not yet arrived to begin their work in the clinic. Samaritan House's

elementary school was not in session, so there were no children about, and the house was unusually quiet. Vi and Professor Raymond went to the large room that served as a meeting and dining area and included a parlor setting near its main fireplace.

Mark looked intently into Violet's face.

"What do you see?" she asked.

"The face that is dearest to me in all the world," he said softly, without breaking his gaze. "The loveliest complexion, the most beautiful mouth, the firmest chin, the most graceful neck, the elegant brow, the velvety brown eyes. . . No photograph could capture the beauty of what I see. I want to take your image with me, so that I may call it up and comfort myself with the knowledge of what awaits me when I return to India Bay."

"Then smile for me, my love," she said, "for I too wish to engrave your image on my heart. I want to think of you always smiling."

She was instantly rewarded, and her heart seemed to skip a beat as his face was transformed by the slightly lopsided smile that she so loved.

"I will miss you so much," she said. "But I had a good talk with the Lord this morning, and He told me how to be strong while you are away."

" 'Perfect love drives out fear,' " he said, echoing the very same verse, 1 John 4, that had inspired and comforted her earlier.

He went to stand at the fireplace, resting an arm on the marble mantel. "I've gone away from you before," he said, "and we have been separated for longer periods. But when I think of the next six weeks, they seem to stretch out before me like years. I won't even have your letters to com-

fort me, for once we leave Mexico City, there will be no friendly postmen to deliver your correspondence."

"I know," Vi sighed. Then her face brightened, and she said, "But there is mail between here and Mexico City! Give me the address of your hotel, and I shall write to you there. You can have my letters waiting when you return to the city after the expedition. I'm sure Max, Lulu, and Gracie will write as well, so a whole mountain of mail can be there for you when you emerge from the jungle."

"That would be wonderful," he said with a grin. "I was worried about the children—that they would become anxious not hearing from me. Leave it to my darling, brilliant Vi to find a solution. Even though I cannot reply, their letters will be a link to me. And your letters—they will be more precious to me than pearls."

"Don't forget that you are to telegraph us as soon as you arrive in New Orleans," she said with mock firmness.

"I won't forget, Miss Travilla," he replied, imitating the voice of a student responding to a teacher.

"Don't tease me," she said seriously.

"I didn't mean to, darling," he said, "but I don't want you to worry. I will be part of a large party of archaeologists, students, and excellent native guides. The leader of our group has explored the area in the past, so we won't be going into unknown territory. I don't expect danger. I do anticipate returning unshaved, disheveled, dirty, and sunburnt." He smiled disarmingly. "You may not even recognize me when you see me next."

"I would recognize you anywhere, no matter how dirty and disheveled," she laughed.

Their privacy lasted some minutes longer, and they talked of several important matters—especially Vi's promise to watch over Mark's children and to assist his housekeeper, Miss Moran, and maid, Kaki Kennon.

"I feel somewhat guilty, leaving you with such responsibility for my household," Mark said. "You already have more work here than most people could handle."

"I don't think of your children and your household as work," Vi said. "You can be fully confident of Miss Moran and Kaki. I doubt they will need much assistance from me. And you know how I feel about the children, how much I love them."

"Still, I worry that—" he began.

Vi cut him off by stepping closer and putting her fingers to his lips.

"Let's agree to remove that word—*worry*—from our minds," she said in a gentle tone. "Our Father in Heaven is watching over us all, and His Word tells us how useless it is to worry over what we cannot control. Let's give over our worries to Him, Mark, in the knowledge that His love is perfect."

He took her hand and held it. "You're right as always, my darling Violet."

He was still holding her hand when Mrs. O'Flaherty bustled in, signaling her entrance with a series of comically loud coughs and sputters.

"What time does your train go, Professor?" the kind lady asked.

"One o'clock," Mark said as he reluctantly dropped Vi's hand. "I have some packing to finish, and I want to spend the rest of the morning with my children. They are being quite brave, but I think they can use some final reassurance."

He looked at Vi and said, "I will tell them about your plan for writing to me."

"Tell them that is *your* plan," Vi said.

Thinking again how wise she was, he said, "I will."

He took Vi's hand again and quickly kissed it. Then he crossed to where Mrs. O'Flaherty stood and said a few words of parting to her. He walked toward the entry hall but turned back at the doorway. His cheeks were flushed and his eyes shone like jewels.

"Farewell, Vi," he said in a voice that cracked with emotion. "My heart is with you always."

He turned again on his heel, and taking long, determined strides, he left the house.

"*Vaya con Dios*," Vi whispered. "Go with God, my love."

Mark was glad he had come to Samaritan House in his carriage. He didn't want to share his emotions with anyone, even a hired cab driver whom he would never see again. He had to get his feelings in check, and the drive across the city provided the time he needed to regain his composure. When he guided the carriage into the drive of his large, comfortable, white house on College Street, he was thrilled to see his children standing on the front porch, lined up like three stair steps.

Max, the oldest at age twelve, waved first. Then Lulu, who was two years younger, raised both her arms and waved vigorously. Gracie, the youngest, was bouncing up and down on her toes in excitement.

Mark reined the horse to a halt. As he alighted, the children clustered around him, and he scooped six-year-old Gracie up into his arms.

"When I get back from Mexico," Mark said to her, "you will probably be too big for me to grab you up and toss you over my shoulder."

Gracie giggled. "I'm getting stronger, Papa," she said, "but not that strong."

"You are all getting stronger," Mark said, as they walked into the house. "Now, who will help me pack my valise?"

"Me!" "Me!" "Me!" the children cried out.

After telling the jovial housekeeper, Miss Moran, that he was home, Mark led the children upstairs to his room. There wasn't much left to pack, but he let the girls fold some shirts while Max collected his shaving items. When the valise was almost full, Gracie got Mark's Bible from his desk and slipped it into the travel case.

"You can read it on the train," she said.

He sat down on the bed, put Gracie on his knee, and motioned to Max and Lulu to sit on either side of him. "I will read it on the train to New Orleans," he said, "and on the ship as we cross the Gulf, and on the train to Mexico City, and at the excavation site. When you three read your Bibles at night before bed, you will know that I am doing the same. It's a way for us to be together even though I'm not here with you. I will read my Bible each night and know that I am with you, and we are all with God. Together, we'll be bound by the Spirit of Christ."

"That's nice, Papa," Gracie said, leaning back to rest her blonde head against his shoulder.

"I wish I could go with you, Papa," said Max.

"Someday, you will," Mark said. "Someday when you are a little older and even stronger than you are today, you will all go with me, and we will have an adventure together."

"Really?" Lulu asked. She often imagined accompanying her father on his travels, but this was the first time he had spoken of such a possibility as if it might actually happen.

"Really," Mark said, "if that is God's plan for us. I want you children to see the world and all the people who share it with us. I also want you to see the work I do when I'm away from you."

"Will Miss Vi come to the railway station today?" Lulu asked cautiously.

"No, dear. I've already said good-bye to Miss Vi and our other friends at Samaritan House," Mark said. "But Miss Vi and Mrs. O'Flaherty are coming here to tea later this afternoon, after you three have seen me off. You will see them quite often this summer, for they've agreed to keep an eye on you and the house."

"Why?" Lulu asked. "We've got Miss Moran and Kaki. They'll take good care of us. And we've got Elwood to tend the stable and the garden. Elwood can fix anything that gets broke."

With a smile, Mark said, "But Elwood only works here four days a week. And Miss Moran and Kaki may need some extra assistance in my absence. Don't forget that both of them are entitled to a day for themselves every week. We don't want to deprive them of their day of rest, do we? I know that Miss Vi wants you to visit Samaritan House, and I believe she has some other ideas for interesting things to do."

"Could we go to her mamma's house again, Papa?" Gracie asked with interest. "To the country? It's such fun there."

"I think that another visit to Ion might be arranged," Mark replied, giving his youngest a playful hug. "I understand that Miss Vi's brother, Mr. Edward, wants to give you riding lessons."

Max's face lit up at this news. He was about to ask when such a visit might take place, but Lulu spoke first.

"I wish you didn't have to go," she said, laying her hand over her father's. "I know you have to, but —"

"If there were an ancient civilization buried in India Bay, I wouldn't have to go to Mexico," Mark said, keeping his tone light. "By the way, I have an idea for a way you can help me. You know that I cannot receive letters in the jungle. But you can still write to me and tell me all about what you are doing here at home."

"What good is that, if you can't get our letters?" Lulu asked.

"Well, you can write to me at the hotel in Mexico City," Mark said. Then he explained how the members of the archaeological team would gather at the hotel to begin their trip to Yucatan and then would return to the hotel for a day or two after the end of their expedition. The hotel would save his letters while he was away, and he would be able to read them on his trip back to India Bay in August.

"When I read your letters, I will feel as if I haven't been so far from you after all," Mark concluded.

"That's great, Papa!" Max exclaimed. "If I learn to ride, I can tell you everything about it."

"Miss Moran can help me write," Gracie said happily. "And maybe Miss Vi will help us, too."

Looking down at Lulu beside him, Mark asked, "Does my plan sound good to you?"

"Yes, Papa," Lulu said. "I'll write to you."

Mark noticed that Lulu's response to his plan lacked the enthusiasm of her brother's and sister's, but he assumed

that Lulu's attitude reflected her anxiety about his immi-
nent departure. Mark thought that he had learned to read
his children's moods quite well, but he couldn't have
guessed what was really on Lulu's mind.

Miss Moran accompanied the Raymonds to the station,
and Elwood Hogg drove the carriage. The children hadn't
been inside the station since their arrival in India Bay a
month earlier. All three were sad that the time for their
father's departure had come, yet they couldn't help being
excited by the activity in the station and around the trains.

The young Raymonds would miss their father greatly
over the next six weeks, and Mark realized that he would
miss them even more. As whistles blew and bells were rung,
he thought about the times he had left them in the past and
how today, for the first time, he truly felt as if he were leaving his heart behind—with his three children and a young
woman in a mission house. But Mark had done an excellent
job of preparing Max, Lulu, and Gracie for this moment, so
the parting was not melancholy. Confident now of his love
for them, all three were equally confident of his return.

Still, when Mark finally stepped into the passenger car,
Gracie's cheeks were damp with soft tears, and Max's chin
trembled as he struggled not to cry. Even Miss Moran had
to resort to her handkerchief to dab away her tears. Only
Lulu's eyes were dry, but had anyone been paying attention, they would have seen how pale her face had become
when she gave her Papa his good-bye kiss.

On the ride back to College Street, Max and Gracie
talked animatedly about what their father would be doing

in Mexico. Miss Moran asked lots of questions to keep the children occupied, and it pleased her to see how proud the young Raymonds were of their father and his work. Lulu took part in the conversation, though Miss Moran noticed that the girl seemed unusually distracted. But that was only natural, Miss Moran thought, and she was sure Lulu would soon snap out of it.

Not even Max—who understood Lulu better than anyone—could have imagined what Lulu was thinking. A couple of weeks earlier, she had devised a plan to keep her family together, forever. Just her father and Max and Gracie and herself—*nobody else*. Especially not Miss Violet Travilla, who was pretty and kind but could never, in Lulu's mind, take the place of her own beautiful mother, who had died when Lulu was not quite six years old. So Lulu had decided to drive away Miss Vi. Lulu's plan was to be such a naughty child that a nice lady like Miss Vi would surely despise her. *I can't have a stepmother if no one wants to be my stepmother,* Lulu reasoned to herself.

Until this day, however, Lulu's plan had been little more than an idea. *But now,* she thought, *Papa is gone, and Miss Vi is coming for a visit. What can I do? What can I do that will make Miss Vi mad, but won't hurt her? I don't want to hurt her, or anybody. I just want her to get so mad that she'll go away and leave us alone.*

Then she remembered what she had left in the hidey hole.

CHAPTER 2

A Picnic Prank

*A man's wisdom gives him
patience; it is to his glory
to overlook an offense.*

PROVERBS 19:11

A Picnic Prank

*M*iss Vi and Mrs. O'Flaherty were coming at five o'clock, which left plenty of time for Gracie to have a good sleep. After so many years of being undernourished by her misguided Aunt Gert, with whom the children had lived following their mother's death, Gracie did not have the endurance of most children her age and still needed her daily nap.

Max, spotting several of his new friends, went off to play baseball. He asked Lulu to come watch the game—the boys wouldn't let her play—but she decided to help Miss Moran in the kitchen. Miss Moran loved tea parties, and she wanted to make this little gathering very special. She had baked cookies and little cakes that morning. She was also preparing dainty sandwiches, fruit salad, egg tarts, and cold tea and lemonade.

"Isn't this a lot of food for just Miss Vi and Mrs. O?" Lulu asked as she carefully spread butter on slices of bread for the sandwiches.

"Well, it will serve for our supper," Miss Moran said in her merry way. "I think it's pleasant sometimes to have a cold meal, like a picnic. I just hope it doesn't rain, for I'm going to set the tea table under the maple trees."

Lulu finished buttering the bread and asked if she might be excused.

"Of course, dear," Miss Moran said. "Run along and play. I'll call you when it's time to dress."

Lulu hung up her kitchen apron and dashed out the back door. She ran across the yard, past the vegetable garden that Elwood Hogg had planted, around the stable, and through the small pasture. Her face was dripping with per-spiration when she crawled into the shady hideaway under the old boxwood bush at the far end of the pasture. It was like a leafy cave, and it was her favorite place. Max had dis-covered the hidey hole on their first day in India Bay, but he had lost interest in it. No one else came there, so the hidey hole had become Lulu's private sanctuary. Just the day before, she had changed the straw on the dirt floor, so she would have a comfortable bed on which to lie and read or just think.

But this afternoon she had no time for thinking. As her eyes adjusted to the shade, she saw what she was after: a small pasteboard box with jagged holes punched into its sides. Lulu wiggled into a cross-legged position, wiped her wet face and neck with her pinafore, and took the paper box onto her lap. As she untied the piece of string that secured the lid, she felt the box bump and shake. Carefully, she lifted the lid just enough for a peek inside. Two green tree frogs looked back at her. She closed the lid quickly and retied the string.

"I'm going to set you loose," she said, "but you have to do something for me first. Then you can go back to your trees."

Tucking the box under her arm, Lulu scrambled out of the hidey hole and retraced her route back to the house, walking this time and trying not to jiggle the box. At the kitchen door, she heard Miss Moran humming a hymn as she worked. Lulu held the box down at her side, hoping her pinafore would hide it, and entered.

"Back so soon?" Miss Moran asked. She was cutting lemons and didn't look up at Lulu. "You can dress and then wake your sister and help her decide what to wear."

A Picnic Prank

"Yes, ma'am," Lulu said as she slipped through the door into the hallway.

Upstairs in her bedroom, she set the box on her desk. Then she got a shallow dish from her dresser, dumped its contents — hair pins, a few buttons, and a flat pebble — and filled the dish with water. She untied the string, raised the box's lid enough to get her hand in, put the water dish inside, and then tied the string again.

Lulu filled her washing basin and scrubbed her face and arms. She changed her stockings and put on her party shoes. She took a yellow patterned dress from her wardrobe and found the pinafore she wanted, the one with two deep pockets that buttoned closed. She finished dressing quickly, and after waking Gracie, she went down to the kitchen, where Kaki was putting the finishing touches to the party food.

Lulu asked if she could help, and soon she and Kaki were carrying linens, plates, and silverware out to the table Elwood had set up under the largest of the three maple trees in the side yard. Kaki unfurled a white cloth and draped it over the table. Following Kaki's instructions, Lulu laid the table and folded the napkins. Kaki placed a lovely bowl of clear crystal etched with a design of birds and curling vines in the center of the table.

"That's a beautiful piece," Kaki said, admiring the crystal bowl. "The professor said it came all the way from London."

"He got it for Mamma when he was on one of his trips," Lulu said softly. "She kept it on the top shelf of a cabinet in our house."

"You were mighty young to recollect them days," Kaki said.

"I was nearly six when Mamma died," Lulu said. "I remember her."

"Well, you cherish them memories," Kaki said, thinking of her own dear mother, whom she hadn't seen since she came across the ocean from her native Ireland. But being a practical girl, Kaki didn't often indulge in reverie. "I'm gonna snip some flowers," she said, pulling a pair of scissors from her apron pocket and clicking the blades. "You get a jug of water from the kitchen, and we'll make a pretty arrangement in that bowl."

Lulu was glad to attend to more chores. The crystal bowl evoked memories that she didn't want, not today. Deep in her heart, Lulu knew what her mother would think of the trick she was planning. But she wouldn't open her conscience to that knowledge. She wouldn't let herself think about how disappointed her mother would be.

Get the water, she told herself firmly. *Fix the flowers. Talk to Kaki.*

Lulu shut off all thoughts of her mother. She turned deaf ears to the warnings of her conscience. She denied herself the counsel of God's Holy Spirit, which would help her find her way to the path of righteousness. In her determination to follow her plan, Lulu didn't understand that her strong will, which had for so long enabled her to protect her brother and sister and now her father, could be both a blessing and a curse.

Max returned from his ball game just in time to change his clothes and join his sisters and Miss Moran on the front porch. He was still huffing when the buggy from the mission pulled up. The children hadn't seen Vi and Mrs. O'Flaherty in some days, and even Lulu, in spite of herself, responded gladly to the ladies' warm smiles and cheerful greetings. Miss Moran led them to the side yard, where the tea table, surrounded by comfortable wicker chairs, was a splendid sight. Vi was especially impressed by the center-piece—the crystal bowl now overflowing with pink and yellow blossoms, dark green sprays of ivy, and sprigs of aromatic mint—and Miss Moran graciously gave full credit to Kaki and Lulu.

They chatted for a time, and Vi was relieved to see that Max, Lulu, and Gracie did not seem too upset by Mark's departure. On the contrary, the children were excited about their father's bold adventure.

"Papa said we can go with him someday when we're stronger," Gracie bubbled.

"He did?" Mrs. O'Flaherty asked in surprise. "Where would you like to go?"

Gracie's brow wrinkled as she thought. Then she exclaimed, "The South Pole!"

"It's too cold there," Max said. "It's all ice and snow. Nobody goes there."

"Cold?" Gracie said in puzzlement. "But it's south. So it's got to be warm and sunny, like India Bay."

Max tried to explain, but Gracie just didn't see how the South Pole could be covered with ice. So Vi suggested they go to the library, where she knew there was a large globe of the world.

"A very good idea," Miss Moran said. "Then you chil-dren can show our guests the garden."

Vi and Mrs. O'Flaherty followed the children to the library. They gathered around the globe, which was encased in a wooden floor stand. It took some minutes, but Max finally convinced his little sister that the South Pole was indeed very cold and desolate.

"I don't want to go there!" Gracie declared.

"How about here?" Vi asked, turning the globe and pointing to an area closer to the equator. "This is the Mediterranean Sea, where it is warm and sunny. Here is the country of Greece," she went on, moving her finger. "And here is Egypt, the land of the pharaohs, and this is the Holy Land, where our Lord lived. Your father has been to all those places."

"What's that funny thing?" Gracie asked, pointing to a long, thin peninsula that jutted into the blue of the sea. "It looks like a lady's boot, the kind with a high heel."

"That's Italy," Mrs. O'Flaherty said. "See that black dot? That's Rome, where Miss Vi's big sister lives." She twisted the globe and pointed to some islands far to the north of Italy. "These are the British Isles, and here is Ireland, where Kaki and I were both born."

Twisting the globe again, Mrs. O asked, "Can you tell me where your father will be in a few days?"

Max plunked his finger down on a tiny curl of land in the Gulf of Mexico. "This is Yucatan, at the bottom of Mexico."

"Is it warm in Yucatan?" Gracie wondered.

"Papa says it's hot, lots hotter 'n India Bay," Lulu replied.

Gracie earned a laugh when she said, "That's where I want to go, where it's hot."

"Then let's go to your garden," Mrs. O'Flaherty said. "We know it's hot in our Southern sun."

A Picnic Prank

They left the library, but Lulu excused herself at the front door, saying she needed to wash her hands before tea. As soon as the others were gone, Lulu raced upstairs to her room. She washed her hands in her basin because she'd said she would. Then she opened the box that rested where she'd left it on her desk and quickly put one frog into a pocket of her pinafore. She repeated this with the other frog and the other pocket.

Down in the kitchen, she found Miss Moran holding a frosty pitcher of lemonade. When Lulu asked if she could help, Miss Moran motioned to a small tray. "Everything else is on the table," the housekeeper said. "If you bring that sandwich tray, we will be ready to eat. Oh, put a towel over the sandwiches, dear. We don't want to attract flies."

Miss Moran went out, but Lulu lingered briefly. The round tray was stacked with small sandwiches in three layers: watercress sandwiches on the bottom, tomato in the middle, and cucumber on top. It looked like a cake. *Now's my chance*, Lulu thought excitedly. *If I'm real careful, I can move this and then...*

The sandwiches looked almost exactly the same when Lulu finished. She laid a white tea towel over the top of the pile and lifted the tray.

⌒

"Ah, the sandwiches," Miss Moran said when she saw Lulu. "Set the tray over there, near our guests. Then come fill your plate."

Lulu did as she was told, placing the tray closer to Vi than to Mrs. O'Flaherty. The ladies sat at the table, but the children and Kaki were seated on a woven rug on the ground. Lulu took a place on the rug where she could clearly see the sandwich tray.

Lulu bit into an egg tart, but she didn't taste it. Her eyes were riveted on the tray. *Take one!* Lulu thought, as if she could will Vi to remove the towel that covered the sandwiches. But Vi was telling Miss Moran something about the work being done on the shelter, which was being created in Miss Moran's old house near the mission.

Take one now! Lulu shouted in her mind.

As she watched, a hand hovered over the tray, lifted the towel and laid it aside, and reached for one of Miss Moran's pretty little cucumber sandwiches. But it wasn't Miss Vi's hand. It was Mrs. O'Flaherty's!

Lulu almost choked on her tart as Mrs. O plucked up a sandwich. But nothing happened.

"This sandwich is delicious," Mrs. O'Flaherty said after several moments. She took another, and still nothing happened. Then Mrs. O pushed the tray even closer to Vi's place, saying, "You must try one, Vi. They are seasoned so delicately, Miss Moran."

"Thank you," Miss Moran replied. "Some people don't like cucumbers but..."

Lulu heard nothing of what the ladies were saying. Her eyes were glued to the tray. She saw Vi lean forward and lift a sandwich from the center of the stack.

A flash of green exploded from the tray. In surprise, Vi leapt up from her chair, and her plate fell to the ground. Then the second frog hopped out of a hole in the center of the sandwiches and looked around as if questioning the cause of the excitement. Suddenly, it drew back and jumped—arcing through the air and landing with a splash in Miss Moran's glass of tea. Miss Moran, as surprised as Vi, reacted with a yelp.

All the children were standing now, staring wide-eyed at the table and Miss Moran's tea glass. A yellowish green frog — no bigger than Gracie's hand — was sitting on a slice of lemon that floated like a lily pad in the tea glass.

Flustered, Miss Moran said, "What — how — where did *that* come from? Gracious me, *it's a frog*! Oh, dear, Miss Vi! One jumped at you, too. Are you all right?"

Lulu turned her eyes back to Vi, expecting to see someone pale with fear or shaking with rage. But Vi was smiling, and as Lulu watched, Vi began to laugh.

"It seems we aren't the only guests," Vi said. She laughed harder.

Stepping to the table, Vi carefully plucked the little frog from the glass and held him on her palm. "You startled us, Mr. Frog," she said, "but I think we may have scared you even more. We're happy you could join us for tea, but I'm sure you'd prefer a fat fly or a mosquito for your meal."

"I never saw such a tiny thing in all me life," Kaki said in amazement.

"It's a tree frog," Vi said. "I don't think they ever get bigger than three or four inches. They usually live in trees near water — a stream or a pond."

"I've seen some of those frogs at the little fish pond over in Willy Sturgis's garden," Max said, referring to one of his new friends. "But I don't see how they can live in trees. Frogs are slippery, and they don't climb."

Without thinking, Lulu said, "They've got sticky feet. Tree frogs'll stick to your hand, so I guess they can stick on the trees."

"How'd you know that?" Max asked with a questioning glance at his sister.

"I—I—maybe I read it somewhere," Lulu replied in confusion. She looked down at her feet, and so she didn't see Vi's gaze upon her.

"Please let him go now, Miss Vi. You'll get ugly warts if you touch him," Gracie said with obvious concern.

"That's just an old tale," Max said dismissively.

"Max is right," Vi said, turning her smile on Gracie. "But so are you, Gracie. I will let him go, for a tree frog is a wild creature. Where is the other one, I wonder?"

They all looked around until Max said, "There, Miss Vi! He's on your chair."

Vi took the second frog from the cushion of the chair. She went to the farthest of the maple trees and set the two unexpected visitors on the ground. In a blink, the frogs were gone. Vi returned to her chair, saying, "Well, that was a nice amusement, but we should finish our tea. I see some tomato sandwiches, and they're my favorite."

Lulu's jaw dropped as Vi took a sandwich from the tray where the frogs had been hidden. Mrs. O'Flaherty took a tomato sandwich and a watercress sandwich as well. Kaki passed the tray to the children, and Max bravely grabbed a tomato sandwich.

"How can you eat that? It's got *frog* on it," Gracie said with a shiver of disgust.

"Aw, it's okay. The frog didn't touch it," Max said. He downed the little sandwich in two bites and took another.

So they all went back to their meal, though Lulu could barely swallow anything. The ladies were conversing as if nothing had interrupted their pleasant afternoon idyll. While Kaki passed Miss Moran's cakes and cookies, Vi asked the children about their activities and also suggested several outings that they might enjoy in the next few weeks. When she mentioned a visit to Ion, Max instantly accepted before remembering to ask Miss Moran's permission, which he received.

Mrs. O'Flaherty reminded the children about the upcoming Fourth of July celebration at Samaritan House. "Perhaps you can come see us tomorrow or the next day," she said. "We have decorations to make, and I could use your assistance. We have just four days left until the party. Do you think you could help me?"

Even Lulu was excited about decorating the lovely old house that was now the mission on Wildwood Street, and Miss Moran always enjoyed visiting the community where she had lived for most of her life. So it was agreed. The Raymond children and Miss Moran would come to Samaritan House bright and early on the day after next, when Elwood could drive them in the carriage.

~

The last rays of the setting sun were painting the horizon in incredible hues of pink, gold, and purple light when Vi and Mrs. O'Flaherty took their leave. The two women were silent until Vi steered the buggy from College Street onto the main road that would take them southward to Samaritan House.

Then Vi said, "I was happy to see that the children are not despondent about their father's departure. After such a busy day, I think they will sleep well tonight."

"Only I suspect that one of them may have a few guilty dreams," Mrs. O'Flaherty replied.

Violet's Defiant Daughter

"Lulu?" Vi asked, though she knew the answer.

"I observed her well, and it was clear to me that she was responsible for the joke," Mrs. O said. A chuckle came into her voice as she went on, "I must admit that it was a good joke, and no one was harmed—not even the poor frogs. It will be quite a while before I forget the sight of that helpless creature in Bessie Moran's tea glass. I thought it likely to be a boy's prank, but Lulu gave herself away with her remark about tree frogs having sticky feet. She'd know that fact from having held them in her own hands."

"It was a good joke," Vi agreed in a light tone. "I remember the twins playing much the same trick on my sister Rosemary and me some years ago, except that my brothers employed a large bullfrog to do their mischief."

"You realize that Lulu directed her mischief toward you," Mrs. O'Flaherty said, the humor gone now from her voice.

"I do," Vi said.

"You have a problem there, Vi," Mrs. O'Flaherty stated plainly. "Max and Gracie adore you, but Lulu. . ." She paused, and when Vi didn't say anything, Mrs. O'Flaherty continued, "I have no doubt that you will ultimately win her affection, but I think you must tread very carefully. Something is tearing at that poor child's heart. Whatever sorrow or pain she is carrying, I do not believe that you are the cause of it, but nevertheless, you are the target of her feelings."

"If only she would trust me, I'm sure I could help her," Vi responded. "This may sound strange, but I feel a special kind of kinship with Lulu. I don't know what she is feeling, yet somehow I do know. It's like when you cannot recall a word or a name that you know perfectly well. It's there, in your mind, but blurred just enough so that you cannot quite read it."

Mrs. O'Flaherty said, "I understand what you mean. You sense the cause of Lulu's distress, but you cannot quite name it. Perhaps you and that young girl have more in common than we suspect. Is it possible that the answer to her behavior may lie somewhere in your own experience? I am praying for you both. God will help you find the key to Lulu's secret. Trust in Him and be patient with that little girl."

"I have faith and patience," Vi said with a sigh. "The trouble is that I have so little time. Just six weeks until Mark returns, and what if. . .?"

Mrs. O'Flaherty threw up her hands and exclaimed, "Now don't you go worrying about 'what if' and 'might be'! That's God's province, and He doesn't need assistance from us mortals. You keep your focus where it belongs—loving those three motherless children and their father—and leave the future to our wise and loving Father in Heaven."

Night had fallen, and Vi was guiding the buggy at a speedy clip through the bright center of the city. In another minute or two, they would leave the city lights behind and enter Wildwood, where the streets were cloaked in shadows.

"I promise to stay squarely in the present," Vi said. "Still, I can't help wondering what Lulu has planned for me when next we see her."

"An apology perhaps," Mrs. O'Flaherty ventured to suggest.

" Maybe," Vi responded softly. "Or maybe something bigger than two tree frogs to test my patience."

CHAPTER

3

Frogs' Tales

*God has brought me laughter,
and everyone who hears
about this will laugh
with me.*

GENESIS 21:6

*L*ulu did not get much sleep that night. What troubled her was not guilt, but the outcome of her joke. It had gone exactly as she'd hoped, with the frogs popping out of the sandwiches. Miss Vi had been startled at first, but then... Lulu had expected Miss Vi to be horrified and upset. Instead, Miss Vi had laughed! And she'd picked up the frogs and set them free! Lulu had been prepared to confess on the spot that the prank was all her doing. That was sure to make Miss Vi very angry. But Miss Vi had laughed! Everybody laughed. Even Lulu herself laughed when she saw the second frog land in the tea. She hadn't confessed after all, because it didn't seem the right thing to do when everyone else was laughing and having a good time.

The worst came later. After Miss Vi and Mrs. O'Flaherty left, Lulu had played for a while outside with Max and Gracie. They'd caught fireflies and kept them in a jar until Miss Moran called them in. Lulu usually loved setting the fireflies free and watching them form a shimmering cloud of pale green light for a second or two before scattering into the darkness. Tonight, this ritual only reminded her of the tree frogs and her failed efforts. Lulu could not understand what had gone wrong with her plan.

Before bed, Miss Moran read to the children, but Gracie had been so tired that she fell asleep in the housekeeper's lap. When Miss Moran took Gracie upstairs, Max also went to his room, but Lulu dawdled in the parlor before going to her own bed.

Lulu hadn't forgotten her promise. Every night she would read her Bible, and her Papa would read his, and it would be as if they were together. She decided on the story of Shadrach, Meshach, and Abednego in the fiery furnace. The story always thrilled her adventure-loving imagination, and she wanted to distract her mind from the events of that afternoon.

She'd just finished the third chapter of the book of Daniel when there was a loud knock at her door, and Max came in. There was a stormy expression on his face, which Lulu knew meant trouble. He shut the door and held out a pasteboard box.

"What's this?" he demanded. "I came in earlier to tell you good night, and I saw this on your desk."

Lulu started to say something, but Max stopped her. "You did it, Lulu," he declared. "You kept the frogs in this box, and you put them in the sandwiches. You wanted to frighten Miss Vi and Mrs. O. What's wrong with you, Lulu? That was a mean thing to do, even if nobody got mad. Papa's trusting us to be good. But he hasn't been away for a full day, and already you've let him down."

Lulu managed to get a word in, saying, "I'm sorry, Max. It was just a little joke. I didn't mean —"

Max slammed the box down on Lulu's dresser. "I know what you meant," he said in a low, angry tone. "You meant to be hateful to Miss Vi. I don't know what you have against her, but all the rest of us like her. Papa likes her. And she likes us. So don't you ever do anything like this again."

Lulu repeated, "I'm sorry."

Max's voice softened a bit: "You don't have to apologize to me, Lulu Raymond. You gotta apologize to Miss Vi and Mrs. O'Flaherty. And to Miss Moran too, for nearly ruining her nice tea party. Don't look at me with that mad face of yours. Promise me that you'll apologize to Miss Moran tomorrow and to the ladies when we go to Samaritan House."

Lulu had never heard her brother so mad before. Tears came to her eyes, and she dropped her head, so Max couldn't see her cry. In a small voice, she said, "I promise, Max. I'll apologize."

She thought that Max might say something nice to her, but he just stalked to her door. "You oughta apologize to God, too," he said. "Pray for Him to forgive you. That's what Papa would tell you to do." Then he left, shutting the door behind him with a bang.

Alone, Lulu began to tremble with emotion. Yes, she would apologize to Miss Vi, but not because she was sorry. If Lulu's plan was going to work, Miss Vi had to know who played the joke. Miss Vi had to think the worst of Lulu.

Now Max is really, really mad at me, and it's all Miss Vi's fault! Lulu sniffed back fresh tears and brushed at her hot cheeks with her hand. *Miss Vi thought it was so funny! Now I've gotta think of something that's not funny. I've gotta show Miss Vi how bad I am, so she won't ever want to be my stepmother. Max will understand when he knows why I'm doing this. I can't let Miss Vi take our Papa from us and make him forget all about our sweet, beautiful Mamma. I just can't let Miss Vi steal his love and ruin our family!*

Lulu usually said a little prayer before she turned out her light, but not tonight. She didn't want to think about God tonight. She didn't want Him to know what she'd done, and she thought He wouldn't know if she didn't tell Him.

She lay down on her bed and pulled the light cotton sheet around her. Squeezing her eyes shut, she tried to sleep. But her mind was whirling. She pictured her father, traveling through the night on a fast-moving train, but the thought of him so far away brought tears to her eyes once more. She turned over and over, but she couldn't find a comfortable position. Her windows were open, but her room seemed stifling hot, and every inch of her skin felt prickly. She punched her pillow, but still it felt as hard as a brick. Nothing made her feel better. It was a very long time before sleep finally came.

The next morning, Lulu made good on her promise to Max. She was more tired when she awoke than she'd been the night before, but she dressed quickly and went down to the kitchen in hope of finding Miss Moran before everyone else came to breakfast. It was with genuine regret that Lulu confessed her prank to the gentle lady. Miss Moran promptly forgave her, saying that the joke was harmless, but also warning Lulu that practical jokes can have unexpected consequences.

"Have you told the Lord what you did?" Miss Moran asked. "Have you asked for His forgiveness?"

"Not yet," Lulu said, lowering her eyes.

"Well, He knows what you did, for He knows all the secrets of our hearts. You need only to ask Him to forgive you. As the Good Book says, He is a 'forgiving God, gracious and compassionate, slow to anger and abounding in love.' And He is never more loving and compassionate than when we open up our hearts and confess our sins to Him."

Lulu suddenly wanted to ask Miss Moran to tell her more about God's love. But Max came into the kitchen, and he glared at Lulu so harshly that she forgot her questions. When Miss Moran left the room for a few minutes, Lulu told Max that she'd made her apology to the housekeeper and had been forgiven.

His expression changed, and he said, "That's good, Lulu. Tomorrow you can tell Miss Vi and Mrs. O'Flaherty that you're sorry. You'll feel better then."

"I feel okay now," Lulu said defensively. But she asked, "Are you still mad at me?"

Max smiled. "Not so much anymore," he said. "But don't do stuff like that again, Lulu. You wanna play catch after breakfast? I'll let you throw my baseball."

Lulu knew that this was Max's way of telling her that he was over being angry, and her spirits climbed. "Can I use your bat, too?" she asked.

~

At Samaritan House, Vi was throwing herself into her work, though Mark and his children were constantly in her mind. There was plenty for her to do. The mission had been in operation for almost one year, and even with the elementary school now on summer vacation, more people were coming in each day. It was Vi's responsibility to see that everything ran smoothly. Currently, her chief interest was overseeing the transformation of Miss Moran's old house into a refuge for people who had no homes.

Until a fire damaged the place the previous winter, Miss Moran had run a boardinghouse there, but she had happily accepted the offer to work for Professor Raymond, and she'd leased her family home to Vi and the mission. The work on the shelter—under the supervision of Mr. Archibald, a master carpenter who had renovated Samaritan House itself the summer before—was proceeding rapidly. Vi felt sure it would be ready for occupation by the end of July.

Vi's duties were changing as the needs of the mission expanded, and she often worked late into the night on her correspondence and bookkeeping. She was also spending more time attending social events with India Bay's well-to-do residents and encouraging them to contribute financially to the mission's work. Vi came from a very wealthy family, and her widowed mother, Elsie, was the mission's most generous benefactor. Vi herself had inherited a substantial income, which had come under her control on her twenty-first birthday just a few weeks earlier. But it was her dream that the mission should be supported by as many people in India Bay as possible.

On the day after the professor's departure, Vi was scheduled to meet with a group of women who were about to further her dream in another way. The group was a kind of women's club, and Virginia Conley Neuville, Vi's cousin, was a member. Virginia and her friends had volunteered to start a nursery—providing daily care for the youngest children of Wildwood. Vi had not been so surprised that Virginia's friends wanted to contribute money. But God's blessing was so much greater: The ladies of the club—wives and daughters of some of the city's most influential citizens—were donating their time to set up and operate the nursery. It was scheduled to open the next week, and the volunteers were coming to discuss last-minute preparations. Vi was arranging chairs in the old storage room off the mission's entry hall when Virginia arrived.

"I'm early," Virginia said as she hugged Vi. "I wanted to get here before the others. I came to prepare you for something that might be—well—a little difficult. Our club has a new member, someone you know, and she's — ah — she's — well — Oh, it's Penelope Pepper, and she wants to help with the nursery. We couldn't say 'no' to her, especially when she made a very large contribution to our day nursery fund."

Vi hardly knew what to say. She did indeed know Miss Pepper, who was the only child of the richest family in India Bay. Miss Pepper was the same age as Vi's big sister, but as unlike sweet Missy as night is from day. Penny Pepper was *bossy*, and she didn't mind using her wealth and social position to get her way.

"Is she planning to work with the children?" Vi asked with a frown.

"I'm sorry to say that's exactly what she plans," Virginia sighed. "Our hope is that she will soon move on to another interest. But there's no predicting her." Then Virginia told Vi just how much Miss Pepper had pledged to donate. It was a huge sum — enough to support the day nursery for a couple of years.

"We'll make do," Vi said with a wry smile. "I must trust our Lord's reasons for sending Miss Pepper to us."

The cousins left the worrisome topic of Miss Pepper and talked of family until the ladies of the club began to arrive. About a dozen women gathered in the old storage room, now painted in a cheerful shade of peach and equipped with all the necessary items for young children — from toys and books to a stack of small mattresses for times of rest. Mrs. Kidd, the wife of a prominent lawyer, was about to call the meeting to order when angry sounds came from the entry hall.

Vi rushed out and found Miss Penelope Pepper towering over an elderly woman and loudly demanding to be directed to "the mistress of this house." Vi quickly took over, greeting Miss Pepper and directing her attention away from the confused old lady.

This is going to be very interesting, Vi thought to herself, as she ushered Miss Pepper into the nursery room.

~~~~~

The next morning, Vi had just finished dressing when young Polly ran into her bedroom, waving an envelope. "A man just brought it!" Polly exclaimed.

Vi instantly saw that it was a telegram. She hurriedly opened the envelope and read the brief message inside. It was from Mark, sent from New Orleans. The trip was going well, he wrote, and he would telegraph again soon. The last line read, "Tell the children I miss them. Will send a long letter soon." That was all, but had it been a lengthy letter of romance, it could not have brought more joy to Vi's heart.

"Is it from the professor?" Polly asked.

"Yes, and he is safely on his journey," Vi replied. Tucking the telegram into her pocket, she said, "Your friend Gracie is coming to visit today."

"I know," Polly said with a glowing smile. "Mrs. O's got lots of work for us—making decorations for our birthday party."

"Birthday party?" Vi asked.

"America's birthday," Polly grinned. "Mrs. O says the United States of America was born on the fourth of July."

"Then your decorations must be very special," Vi said, as she took Polly's hand.

The Raymond children and Miss Moran got to the mission in mid-morning. After greeting everyone and spending a little time with the mission cat, Max, Lulu, Gracie, and Polly accompanied Mrs. O'Flaherty to the empty school-room on the second floor. Mrs. O soon had them cutting paper streamers and coloring paper flags.

Meanwhile, Vi and Miss Moran walked to Miss Moran's old house to inspect the work proceeding there. Miss Moran was impressed by the new kitchen and wash house and the bathing rooms that had been constructed upstairs and down. Mr. Archibald explained how the new water pumping system and coal-fired steam heating worked, and even though Miss Moran didn't understand a word he said, she shared the master carpenter's pride in these modern conveniences.

"Your house can accommodate as many as six families at a time," Vi said, "and even more in an emergency. People may stay for as long as it takes to make permanent arrangements, and we'll do everything we can to help them find homes or jobs."

"It warms my heart to see my old house used for the good of my friends and neighbors in Wildwood," Miss Moran said with a gentle smile.

On the walk back to the mission, Vi asked Miss Moran how the children were adjusting to their father's absence.

"So far, they seem content," Miss Moran said. "Lulu is a little restless, but I imagine that she'll be fine. Has she spoken to you about the incident the other day?"

"The frogs who came to tea?" Vi said with a chuckle. "No, but Mrs. O'Flaherty and I were certain that it was Lulu's little joke."

"She apologized to me yesterday morning, and she intends to talk to you," said Miss Moran. "Perhaps you could find a little private time for her today. She's a proud child, and it might be easier for her to speak if others are not present."

"I'll do that," Vi promised. "Do you think Lulu is overly proud, Miss Moran?"

"Oh, no, not overly so," the little lady demurred. "I believe she is lonely."

"Lonely?" Vi asked. "But she has so many people who love her. Her father, Max and Gracie, Kaki, and you. . ."

"And *you*, Miss Violet," replied Miss Moran in a knowing way. "I have not been with the children long enough yet to be a confident judge of all their feelings. Kaki has told me of their lives before they came here and how the poor darlings suffered, especially from their father's neglect. I don't condemn Professor Raymond, for his own misery and grief were great in those days. He told me how, in his sorrow, he denied himself the comfort of our Heavenly Father's healing love. He said that someone very special and dear to him helped awaken him to the truth and reunite him with his children. Oh, it's a joy, Miss Violet, to see what a good, attentive father he is. But—"

Miss Moran paused. They walked several more steps; then Miss Moran halted and took Vi's arm. "Somewhere inside herself, Lulu is afraid that she will lose her father's love. Maybe it's not my place to say anything, but that little girl is still suffering, and she is deliberately suffering alone. After the professor told me of his struggle to renew his faith, I began to see how much Lulu is like him. She believes in God, but she distances herself from His saving grace. That child is in a lonely place. I don't think it's pride that isolates her; it's fear. If you could help her, the way you helped the professor—"

Miss Moran's eyes flew open. "I—I didn't mean to say that," she stammered quickly. "I don't really know. . ."

"That's all right," Vi said with a warm smile. "I'm not surprised you've guessed about the professor and me, for you are a very perceptive person."

"I won't say anything to the children," Miss Moran pledged. "It's just that I want you to be happy. I want all of you to be happy. I want Lulu to be happy. Our true happiness lies in having the Lord in our hearts, present with us always. Lulu needs help to know Him as we do. Can you help her, Miss Violet?"

"I can try," Vi said thoughtfully. "With God's help, I will try."

"Just don't give up on her, whatever happens," Miss Moran said. Then she laughed softly and said, "She may be a hard nut to crack, but I do believe there's a noble young heart beating inside her. Right now, she seems to be testing us, and she has mischief on her mind. You'll need to have patience with her."

"Patience," Vi said with a sigh. "That's my great weakness. All my life, I've been too impatient and too quick to jump to conclusions. We'll have to pray, Miss Moran, as Paul prayed for the Colossians, that we may have 'great endurance and patience.'"

They walked on, talking about the power of faith to overcome weakness and fear, and Vi felt stronger, knowing that the Lord had given her an ally in Miss Moran. When they reached the mission, they found the children setting a table in the meeting room for the residents' lunch. Mrs. O'Flaherty was at her piano playing "Yankee Doodle," and Max and the girls were singing as they worked.

Violet's Defiant Daughter

After their mid-day meal, Mrs. O'Flaherty invited Miss Moran to join the children and her as they finished the holiday decorations. "Would you like to help us?" Mrs. O asked Vi. "We still have some bunting banners to sew."

"I have some business to attend to first," Vi replied. She turned to the children, saying, "May I borrow Lulu for a few minutes? I have something for her."

Lulu felt a little shock of suspicion. *What does Miss Vi want with me? Why just me?* The only way to find out was to follow Miss Vi. When they entered Vi's cozy office, Lulu looked around for Jam, who was usually perched on the window ledge.

Vi sat down in her desk chair and said, "Jam's probably in the cellar. She has found a cool corner, and she retreats there in the afternoon to escape the heat."

"Oh," was all that Lulu could think to say. To avoid looking at Vi, she let her eyes travel slowly about the room. She heard a rattling sound, but didn't shift her gaze until Vi said, "I have this telegram for you. It came early this morning. I thought you should share it with Max and Gracie."

Lulu finally looked at Vi, who was holding out a piece of paper. Lulu took the telegram. "It's from Papa!" she said. "He's well, and he misses us. He's gonna send us a long letter."

Lulu read the telegram again and said, "It's very short. Are all telegrams short like this?"

Vi smiled and said, "I believe they are. Telegrams come much faster than letters, but I'd rather have a letter."

"We're going to write letters to Papa," Lulu said, forgetting her earlier suspicions. "We'll send them to a hotel in Mexico, so he can read 'em when he gets back from the expedition. It was Papa's idea. I'll start my first letter tonight and tell him we got his telegram."

"You might also tell him about the decorations you made today. Mrs. O said she'd never get everything done without your hard work."

"It's fun, Miss Vi. We have a good time with Mrs. O. Did you hear her play the piano? I didn't know she could play like that. She's got a children's choir, and Polly sings in it. Did you know that?"

"I did, and you can hear them sing on Independence Day," Vi said. "I'm counting on you to be here for the celebration," Vi went on. She realized that she had never before spent more than a few minutes alone with Lulu. Her visits had been with all the children. Lulu had been standoffish when they came into the office, but in her now shining face, Vi could see no sign of the loneliness Miss Moran described.

"Do you have lots of parties here?" Lulu asked.

"Well, we had a party on the day when we put the elevator into service, but we hadn't planned to. People just came to see the elevator go up and down, and it turned into a party. Usually, the people who live here in Wildwood don't have the time or money for parties."

"How 'bout birthday parties?" Lulu asked.

"Not even those. Have you ever had a birthday party?" asked Vi.

"I think maybe I did, before we lived with my Aunt Gert. But Aunt Gert said it was vain to have parties for ourselves. I wanted a party when I was ten, but we were still in Boston then. We had a little party for Gracie after we went to live with Papa in Kingstown. Papa got her a cake and presents, and it was really nice."

"I don't think parties are vain," Vi said. "You know, Lulu, God wants us to be joyful and to celebrate His gift of life to us. In Psalm 149, we're told to praise His name with dancing and make music to Him with tambourines and harps."

"That's in the Bible?" Lulu questioned.

"It is," Vi replied. "Your Aunt Gert was not completely wrong, though. Vanity is not good, because it makes us selfish and thoughtless of others. But God wants us to celebrate life, and when we do, we celebrate Him, the giver of life. Tell me, Lulu, when is your birthday?"

"In February," Lulu replied.

"I'll remember," Vi said. "And I'll remember that you like cake and presents."

"That would be really nice of you," Lulu said, her eyes full of sparkle and her smile as sweet as any Vi had ever seen.

"Let's go upstairs now. You can show that telegram to your brother and sister," Vi said, "and I can sew bunting for Mrs. O."

Vi started to rise, but Lulu grabbed her hand. In a frantic rush of words, Lulu said, "It was me, Miss Vi! I put the frogs in the sandwiches! I wanted to scare you, but it was a bad thing to do. A big, dumb joke. I'm so sorry. Can you— will you forgive me?"

Vi pulled her close and said, "Yes, I forgive you. It is brave of you to apologize, and it wasn't such a terrible joke. No one was harmed, but sometimes jokes don't go as we plan, and people can be hurt. Can I tell you something my father taught me when I was about your age?"

"Yes, please," Lulu said in a soft voice.

"It all started when my twin brothers, Harold and Herbert, decided to play a trick, like your joke, on my little sister, Rosemary, and me. They'd found a huge bullfrog in a creek near our house and hid it in a toy box where we kept our picture puzzles. They knew Rosemary and I played with the puzzles every day. When we opened the toy box, that big bullfrog leapt out and smacked poor Rosemary, who was only three years old, in the chest. It knocked the breath right out of her, and she fell to the floor. When their joke went wrong, the twins were so ashamed. They told our Papa what they'd done, and after he forgave them, Papa gave us all a stern lecture about practical jokes. He said something I've never forgotten. He said that a joke is something to share with others. He said that playing a practical joke is like telling a lie because it requires hiding the truth and being deceitful. Papa said that a practical joker always hurts himself more than anyone, because he is breaking his trust with God."

Lulu edged closer to Vi and said, "I don't want to make God mad at me. Max told me to apologize to God, but I don't know how."

"Tell Him what you told me," Vi said. "You can talk to God just like you talk to me or Max or your Papa. He's your friend, the very best friend you will ever have."

Lulu hesitated for a few seconds; then she shut her eyes and said, "I'm sorry, God. I played a dumb trick to scare Miss Vi, and I'm really sorry, and I want to do better. I hope You can hear my apology, 'cause I don't want You to be mad at me."

Lulu opened her eyes and looked at Vi. "Was that right? Do you think God heard me?" Lulu asked.

Violet's Defiant Daughter

"I know He heard you," Vi said, "and if you listen with your heart, He will answer you in His way and in His time. It was a very good prayer."

Lulu still held Vi's hand, though she stepped away a little. "What happened to your little sister? Was she hurt bad?" she asked.

Remembering, Vi grinned and said, "After Rosemary got her breath back, she sat up and started screaming until her face turned as red as a radish. I'd never heard such loud screams. I thought she'd scream the house down. Papa came running, and that's when the twins confessed to him. The instant Rosemary saw Papa, she stopped yelling and started smiling like the cat that swallowed the canary. After that day, we all knew not to make Rosemary screaming mad."

Lulu was giggling, but she had one more question: "What became of the frog?"

Without letting go of Lulu's hand, Vi stood up. "That old bullfrog?" Vi said as she guided the little girl out of the office. "Apparently, Rosemary's chest was harder than his head. She never even got a bruise, but the poor old frog was knocked out cold. I saw him on the floor and scooped him up. I was afraid he was dead, and I carried him outside. By then, he'd started to wriggle in my hands, so I took him to a birdbath in the garden and put him beside the water. His head popped up, his eyes rolled, and his throat started to puff up like a balloon. Then he let out a croak that was almost as loud as Rosemary's screams, and he jumped off the birdbath. The last I saw of him, he was hopping away as fast as he could go toward the creek. Afterward, I used to imagine that when we heard the frogs at night, our Mr. Bullfrog was telling all his friends about his adventure and warning them to stay far, far away from those crazy Travilla children who lived in the big house."

They were almost at the top of the front stairway by now, and Lulu was laughing so hard that she had to stop and clasp her side. Lulu's laughter was infectious, and Vi began to laugh with her. A woman, sitting in the second-floor hallway outside the clinic, witnessed this strange behavior, and then she started to laugh. A few seconds later, Dr. Bowman stepped out of the clinic door, and before he saw Vi, he demanded, "What is this racket?"

"Miss Vi told me a funny story 'bout a bullfrog," Lulu managed to say, before another fit of giggles overcame her.

"A bullfrog, Miss Travilla?" the young doctor said, keeping his voice firm and professional, though his cheeks were twitching with amusement.

"Yes, a story about a bullfrog," Vi replied. She drew in a large gulp of air and seemed in control of herself at last. "And every word of it is true."

Vi and Lulu went on toward the classroom. Looking at their backs, the doctor shook his head from side to side, then turned his attention to his waiting patient and escorted the woman into the clinic. A last burst of feminine giggles came from the hallway as he closed the clinic door.

A Glorious Fourth

Remember the wonders he has done, his miracles, and the judgments he pronounced.

1 CHRONICLES 16:12

A Glorious Fourth

*L*ulu's head and heart were in a spin. She was being pulled in two opposite directions and feeling very unsure of herself. Lulu didn't like being uncertain. But she found herself questioning her ideas about Miss Vi and wondering how she could be so mean to someone who was so kind.

Lulu had assumed all along that Miss Vi was a good person. *Papa wouldn't want to be her friend if she wasn't good,* Lulu reasoned. *She's good and kind and nice to everybody. She works really hard, and she's awfully pretty, but not as pretty as our Mamma. She's funny too. I didn't imagine she'd be funny.*

Thinking about the good times she and her brother and sister had enjoyed at the mission over the last few days, Lulu couldn't contain her smile. Slipping her feet into her boots, she laced them tightly. Then she donned the freshly pressed white linen dress that Miss Moran had laid out on her bed.

Maybe Miss Vi is just a friend, a good friend, to Papa, Lulu thought as she brushed the tangles from her wild, blonde hair. *Maybe I have it all wrong, and Miss Vi just wants to be our friend too. That would be nice. Max says Papa needs friends, and so do we. So maybe it's okay to be Miss Vi's friend, but I don't want to be anybody's daughter 'cept my Papa's.*

Then a dark and defiant thought struck Lulu: *Just don't get too friendly. Some people seem all nice and sweet, like Aunt Gert was when we went to live with her. Then they turn mean and hateful, like Aunt Gert did. Maybe Miss Vi is just acting nice, trying to impress Papa. Oh, why can't Miss Vi be ugly and mean and miserable to everybody, like I used to imagine! Why can't she be like a*

Violet's Defiant Daughter

nasty old witch! Then I wouldn't be confused. I hate not knowing what to think! I just hate —

Her brush snagged on a particularly large tangle, and Lulu yelped, "Ouch!" just as her bedroom door swung open and Gracie skipped in, asking, "What's wrong?"

"My hair," Lulu replied sullenly. The hair brush was caught in the tangle. But the more she pulled, the tighter the brush stuck, and each pull brought a sharp pain to her scalp, tears to her eyes, and another "Ouch!"

"Why can't I have hair like yours?" Lulu wailed. "You got those silky curls, Gracie, like our Mamma's. All I got was a head of dry straw and cockleburs!"

"Stop pulling," Gracie said. "Let Miss Moran brush your hair. She's coming with our new sashes."

Sure enough, Miss Moran walked in a few seconds later and saw Lulu's dilemma. She laid two colorful satin sashes on a chair and immediately set about gently rescuing Lulu's hair. It took some minutes to smooth out the tangles and wrestle Lulu's thick tresses into a neat braid and secure a red satin ribbon at the top end of the long braid.

"The ribbon matches your sash, Lulu," Miss Moran said. "You get the red sash, and the blue is for Gracie. You'll be charming Fourth of July girls today, all decked out in red, white, and blue, like our flag. It's fortunate that the Fourth falls on a Friday this year. Some of the mills and businesses in India Bay have agreed to close early today, and more of the working people of Wildwood may be able to attend."

"Isn't this a holiday for everybody?" Lulu asked, forgetting her earlier thoughts about Miss Vi.

"Not everybody, I'm afraid," Miss Moran said. "Poor working people have little control of their time, and they must often labor, so others can rest and enjoy themselves."

"That's not fair," Lulu protested.

"Well, be that as it may, the party at the mission this afternoon will be a first for the people of Wildwood. No one ever organized such a celebration in the neighborhood before — not until Miss Violet thought of it. I don't think you girls can know how much good that young lady and Mrs. O'Flaherty and their friends have done for Wildwood."

"Papa says Miss Vi got you to come and live with us," said Gracie, lacing her fingers into Miss Moran's.

"Indeed she did," Miss Moran smiled, "and I haven't been so happy in years."

"Us too," Gracie said sweetly.

"We've got lots to celebrate today," Lulu added, taking the housekeeper's other hand, "like having you and Kaki to take care of us."

A tear had come to Miss Moran's eye, but she blinked it away and said, "Come now, and let's hurry along. We promised to get to the mission early, and Kaki is waiting downstairs with the baskets of pies we made. Shall we go?"

Samaritan House was already being dressed up for the celebration when the Raymonds' carriage pulled into the driveway. The railing around the front porch and all of the front windows were adorned with the striped red, white, and blue bunting that Vi and Mrs. O'Flaherty had sewn, and a large American flag hung above the mission door. Under the trees on the garden side of the old house, a number of tables stood in the shade.

Christine was on the porch, sweeping. Little Jacob, wearing a triangle-shaped hat of red paper, was amusing himself by marching up and down the front steps. They stopped to greet the new arrivals.

Looking up at the young man in the driver's seat, Christine said, "Good to see you, Elwood. Your daddy and brothers are out back, and so's my Enoch. He'll stable your horse. I think he could use some help bringing the benches and chairs outside."

Elwood said, "Well, Miz Christine, between Max and me, we got four hands and two strong backs. I 'spect we can be of some assistance."

As the carriage rolled away, Vi came out of the front door to greet Miss Moran, Kaki, and the girls. "You are right on time," Vi said. "Thank you for volunteering to help. The day is so beautiful, and I think we're going to have lots of guests. Miss Moran and Kaki, would you mind helping Mary in the kitchen? The ladies from the churches are preparing the food baskets for delivery to our shut-in neighbors, and Mary has more than she can manage with the food baskets and our picnic."

"Maybe these pies will be useful," Kaki said, nodding at the two baskets suspended over her strong arms.

"Pies? Oh, how splendid," Vi exclaimed. "Mary was just saying that we might not have enough desserts. Here, let me carry one of the baskets. They look heavy."

"A might heavy," Kaki said, allowing Vi to take one of the baskets. It still amazed the young housemaid that a 'high-born' lady like Miss Travilla was always so ready to do what Kaki considered to be servants' chores. But during the two weeks she'd stayed at the mission, before the Raymonds came to India Bay, Kaki had learned that Violet Travilla simply made no distinctions between herself and anyone else.

"What should we do, Miss Vi?" Gracie asked.

Vi replied, "I believe that Mrs. O'Flaherty and Polly need you in the schoolroom, Gracie. They are going to hang the paper streamers that you children made."

"What can I do?" Lulu questioned a little uncertainly. Part of her wanted to stay with Miss Vi. . .and part of her — the scared and defiant part — didn't.

"I have quite a long list of tasks, and I don't believe I can accomplish them all by myself," Vi said. "Lulu, would you be my assistant today?"

In spite of her mixed feelings, Lulu was pleased. "Yes, ma'am," she said with a wide smile, "I'll be your assistant."

Soon, everyone was at their tasks. Gracie joined Mrs. O and Polly in the schoolroom, where they were braiding the crepe-paper streamers into long ropes of red, white, and blue. In the kitchen, Kaki lightened Mary Appleton's load by taking over the job of making gallons of potato salad for the picnic. Miss Moran helped the other ladies — all wives of the ministers of Wildwood's churches — fill baskets for the Wildwood residents who were too ill or aged to attend the picnic.

Meanwhile, Vi and Lulu began carrying boxes and baskets filled with plates, napkins, and other supplies to the tables in the garden.

"What's that good smell?" Lulu asked, sniffing a faint but pungent aroma.

"That's our picnic," Vi said, "or a big part of it. Elwood's father is our butcher, and he has provided a whole hog for our feast. He and Elwood's two older brothers, Lynwood and Dagwood, made a cooking pit in the back garden, and they're roasting the pig over the fire. It's called 'barbecue,' and it takes hours to cook. Mr. Hogg was here at the crack of dawn to start the fire. He tells me that barbecue is quite an art."

"It sure smells good," Lulu commented. Then she giggled.

"Share the joke," Vi said with a smile.

"Mr. Hogg is cooking a hog!" Lulu said, bursting into laughter.

Vi chuckled and said, "I hadn't thought of that. Oh, but we mustn't make fun of someone's name."

"I know," Lulu said, stifling her laugh and feeling a little guilty. "A person can't help having a funny name, and I don't guess it's funny to them."

"Mr. Hogg probably doesn't mind, for he's a very good-natured man," Vi said. "But it's never kind to jest about a person's name or how they look or how they dress, is it? In the Bible, we're told that God doesn't judge anyone by external appearances."

Lulu began folding squares of white cotton into napkins. Then she said seriously, "We can never be as good as God, can we? No matter how hard we try, we can never be that good."

"Only God is perfect," Vi said. "He understands with great compassion how weak and imperfect we are."

"So we can never be perfect?" Lulu asked.

"Not on our own. That's why God sent His Son, Jesus, as our Savior—to be perfect for us. We will still struggle with sin and make mistakes, but His death on the Cross has wiped out the penalty of our sins, and He gives us strength in our weaknesses."

"Miss Vi," Lulu asked after several moments had passed, "do you think a person can do bad things for good reasons? Would God know that the person had good reasons?"

Vi stared at Lulu. She sensed that the little girl was thinking of something specific and personal, and she wanted to reply in a way that might help Lulu with whatever troubled her.

"I think that a person may believe that she, or he, has good reasons," Vi said slowly. "But if in her heart she knows that she's doing wrong, then even good reasons for doing something bad can't excuse the bad deeds. To be honest, Lulu, I can't think of anything really good that comes from doing bad. Let's say that I wanted to have something beautiful, like a great painting or a fabulous jewel, but I didn't have any money and the only way I could get it was to cheat other people to get the money. How do you think I'd feel about that beautiful painting or jewel after I bought it?"

Lulu said quickly, "You're a good person, and you'd feel bad because you'd done a bad thing."

"Thank you for the compliment," Vi said, smiling softly. "And you'd feel bad as well, because there's a strong conscience inside that pretty head of yours. Our conscience is one of God's gifts to us. It tells us what is right and what is wrong. My Papa said that God communicates with us in many ways and that our conscience is one of them. He said I should always listen to my conscience, for it speaks to me of what I need to hear."

Lulu didn't say anything else, but she had a great deal to ponder. As Lulu continued folding the napkins, Vi went back into the house for more boxes. When she returned, she said, "We'll finish unpacking these later. I just passed Doctor Bowman in the hallway, and he said we can help him hang the streamers in the trees."

"Mrs. O'Flaherty told us that you might put up paper lanterns," said Lulu.

Violet's Defiant Daughter

"We considered that. Lights in the trees would be very pretty after sunset," Vi said. "Someone also suggested a fireworks display, but I had to say 'no.' It has been so dry recently that the risk of fire is just too great. So we'll use oil lanterns to light the evening, and Mrs. O'Flaherty's musical program will provide our entertainment."

Lulu looked thoughtful; then she said almost to herself, "You decided on safe ways to do something good. It's going to be a fun party, Miss Vi," she added happily.

Vi put her arm around Lulu's shoulder and said, "I surely hope so."

The picnic was to begin at four o'clock—the regular time for the mission's daily meal—but Vi's family and Alma Hansen arrived from Ion about an hour earlier. Vi greeted her mother, sister, and brothers warmly and quickly assigned tasks to the younger Travillas. Without being asked, Alma hurried away to the kitchen to help Mary, and Elsie followed, in search of Christine.

Ed lifted a valise and several hat boxes from the carriage. "These are Miss Hansen's," he said. "Mamma's friends were thrilled by her designs and commissioned a goodly number of dresses. I have an idea that Miss Hansen could make a profitable business of dressmaking here in India Bay, once the ladies of the city see the gowns she's creating for their country cousins."

"Speaking of country cousins," Vi said, "I thought Zoe might be with you."

"Zoe," Ed replied archly, "decided to accompany Grandpapa and Grandmamma to Aunt Rosie's party."

"That was good of her," Vi said, taking one of the boxes and walking with Ed to the house. "But I miss Zoe. It's been weeks since I've seen her."

"It's been almost as long since any of us laid eyes on her," Ed said. "Her social calendar is too full for us."

"You haven't talked to her yet?" Vi asked.

"No," Ed said in a flat tone that Vi read correctly. Her brother did not want to talk about his feelings for Zoe Love, his grandfather's ward. Vi knew better than to pursue the matter, and she quickly changed the subject.

Elsie Travilla had brought fresh flowers from her garden, and in the meeting room, she and Christine were arranging them into bouquets to grace the picnic tables.

"I thought Ben and Crystal were coming," Christine said, "and bringing the Evans girls. Miss Elsie, I sure do miss having Tansy and Marigold around here."

"They were planning to come, but there's going to be a celebration in the quarters this evening, and Tansy has a speaking part in the Independence Day play that the children are doing," Elsie explained. "But they will come and visit the mission soon. I can't thank you and Enoch enough for helping us decide to bring those children to live at Ion. With Rosemary and Danny growing up, I have a renewed sense of purpose with Tansy and Marigold to teach and nurture. I understand now why grandparents dote so on their grandchildren," she added with a lilting laugh.

"When do you think you'll be seein' that grandbaby boy of yours?" Christine asked, referring to the young son of Elsie's eldest daughter, Missy, and her husband, Lester Leland.

Elsie didn't try to hide the wistfulness she felt: "I hope to travel to Rome next spring, and God willing, I shall see my grandson before he reaches manhood. I can't deny that I wish Lester and Missy would return to the United States to live, but I will leave that to the Lord to decide. Their path is His path, and I don't question His wisdom."

"Maybe you'll be getting some grandbabies closer to home before long," Christine said playfully.

"That is a possibility," Elsie replied, returning Christine's smile, "but we mustn't speak of it."

"No, ma'am," Christine said in a hushed tone. "Nobody 'round the mission speaks a word about it. Still, we can't help thinking it over. Not when it involves the happiness of a young lady we all love like our own."

Outside, Danny Travilla had gone to help Enoch and Max. Enoch was pounding a metal stake into the ground near the mission's storage shed at the rear of the house. It was to be the site for games of horseshoes. Max and Danny were putting checkerboards and boxes of checkers on some tables. When they finished, Enoch sent them to the stable. "Fetch out those horseshoes, boys, while I mark off the pitch. Then go find Mr. Edward. It's gonna take all of us to move Mrs. O'Flaherty's piano out on the porch."

Raising his voice, Enoch called out to a tall, burly man who was working over a smoking hole dug into a bare patch at the far side of the garden. "You gonna have time for a game of horseshoes, Mr. Hogg?"

"You betcha!" Mr. Hogg yelled out. "Soon's we get this pig served up to the folks. How 'bout you and me teaming up against my three boys."

"Think they're a match for us?" asked Enoch.

"Not half a match!" Mr. Hogg shouted gleefully. "They got youth, but you and me's got experience, Enoch. I'll take experience every time."

A Glorious Fourth

The hands of the clock were approaching four when men, women, and children from the neighborhood began to arrive, and soon the mission grounds were ringing with the sounds of people at play. Mothers and grandmothers gathered under the trees to chat while they tended the babies and watched over the small children. At Dr. Bowman's suggestion, some of the elderly men retreated to the rear garden and occupied the checker tables. A gaggle of curious boys followed their noses and went to the back garden to marvel at the huge pig, suspended on an iron spit over the barbecue pit. A cluster of older girls sat about on the front porch, enjoying this rare break from the grindingly hard work of their daily lives. It wasn't often that the residents of Wildwood had the freedom to enjoy themselves.

The church wives, who had returned after their deliveries, and the ladies of the mission began carrying the picnic food from the kitchen to the garden.

"Can't we lend you a hand, Miss Violet?" asked Mrs. Pleasance, a young mother holding a bright-eyed infant on her lap.

Vi set a large bowl on the table, and then she gently touched the baby's downy cheek with a finger. He clasped her finger and gurgled. "You're our guest today, Mrs. Pleasance," she said, "and you must promise me that you will just relax and have a good time. Is Mr. Pleasance coming?"

"Soon's he can, Miss Violet," the young mother said. "His shift at the mill ain't over till five o'clock, and then he's gotta walk back here, unless he can hitch a ride."

Vi excused herself and went to the house. Her steps slowed as she considered the young father who worked ten hours a day, six days a week, in a cotton mill and earned so little that he couldn't spare a few pennies a week to ride the streetcar. Vi's brow darkened as her thoughts traveled to a hillside mansion on the opposite side of town. In that majestic house, amid the finest furnishings that money could buy, lived Prentice Pepper, who owned the mill. *Does Mr. Pepper have any idea how his employees must struggle for their families?* Vi wondered. *Does he —*

Her rumination was cut off by a hearty shout of "Barbecue's ready!" Vi looked up to see Mr. Hogg and his three sons carrying large platters of steaming meat to the picnic tables. A crowd of laughing boys followed close behind.

"Whoopee!" came a gravelly voice from amid the women. Vi spotted the Widow Amos, one of her favorite neighbors, ensconced in a high-backed wicker chair. Mrs. Amos was clapping her gnarled hands. Seated at the old woman's feet were Gracie and Polly, and they, too, began to clap. The other adults and children joined in the spontaneous round of applause, and the butcher beamed with pride.

A hand grasped Vi's shoulder and Ed Travilla said, "Better get this party started, little sister. Nobody's going to wait much longer when everything smells so delicious."

Reminded of her hostess duties, Vi hurried back to the tables. She raised her hand, and all the talk ceased. "We're so happy that so many of our friends could join us to celebrate our country's birthday," she began. "The United States is one hundred and eight years old today."

The Widow Amos clapped and called out, "And she's looking mighty good for her age!"

"Indeed she is," Vi agreed with a dimpled smile. "We have a patriotic program prepared —" she paused, anticipating the groans that arose from some of the younger guests. "But that's for later," Vi continued. "Reverend Stephens will say grace over our table, and then I hope you have good appetites."

A Glorious Fourth

Heads were bowed, and the minister offered a prayer of gratitude for the opportunity to share such a glorious day with friends and celebrate God's generous gift of freedom for all. He asked the Lord's blessing upon the good people in Wildwood and the mission and its work. Then he closed with a request for the Lord to continue to bestow His blessings upon the nation and all its people, near and far.

When Reverend Stephens finished, Vi said, "Please, come fill your plates." The guests came forward, and the picnic began.

～

When Vi finally got her own plate, she realized that she was very hungry. She treated herself to a generous serving of Mr. Hogg's barbecue, a buttery ear of boiled corn, salad, and cornbread. Then she went to join Rosemary, Lulu, and the group of teenage girls on the mission's wide porch. As she was mounting the steps, however, the crunching sound of wheels on gravel caused her to turn her head sharply. Coming through the mission gates was a small but elegant open carriage with a liveried driver at the reins. There was only one passenger—a tall woman in a feathered bonnet sitting ramrod straight in the rear seat. She was dressed in a fashionable but rather severe summer suit of silvery gray silk.

Oh, no! What is she doing here? Vi asked herself. *Just when things were going so well.*

Though her thought was uncharacteristically ungenerous of her, Vi's behavior was impeccable. With her plate still in hand, Vi retreated down the steps and went to greet the last person she expected to see in Wildwood on the Fourth of July.

CHAPTER

5

Pepper, Pies, and Patriotism

*They will celebrate your
abundant goodness and
joyfully sing of your
righteousness.*

PSALM 145:7

Pepper, Pies, and Patriotism

*hat a pleasant surprise," Vi said with all the enthusiasm she could muster, as the carriage driver handed Miss Penelope Pepper down from her vehicle. "I didn't expect to see you until Monday, when the nursery opens."

Miss Pepper nodded ever so slightly at Vi and said, "When I heard you discussing this, ah, event the other day, Violet, I thought I should come and assist."

Then, without turning her gaze from Vi, Miss Pepper spoke to her driver in a commanding tone: "Ralph, take the carriage to the rear and wait. I do not know how long I shall be needed here, so keep the horse in harness."

"Yes ma'am, Miss Pepper," the driver replied meekly.

Seeing the young driver's sweating face above the starched collar of his formal uniform, Vi said, "There's a shady spot under the trees, Ralph. And while you're waiting, please partake of our barbecue picnic and lemonade."

"May I, Miss Pepper?" the driver asked.

With obvious irritation, the lady said, "I suppose, if you attend to your duties." Waving her hand in a dismissive way, as if she were swatting a troublesome insect, she added, "Go now, Ralph. Be ready when I call."

Even before the driver was out of earshot, Miss Pepper said, "Ralph is merely a footman, but our driver is engaged in some chores today. Most inconvenient."

"Well, it's so nice that you are here," Vi said, trying to make her words sound sincere. "Come and have some barbecue. It is really delicious."

Looking down at Vi's full plate, Penny Pepper wrinkled her nose and said, "I have already dined, thank you. I see you have a large rabble to feed."

"Hardly rabble," Vi said sweetly. "These are our neighbors and friends. In fact, a number of the small children you see with their mothers will be coming to our day nursery next week. Would you like to meet them?"

Looking toward the picnickers, Miss Pepper raised her chin several degrees and sniffed, "Hardly necessary, Violet. I shall meet the poor, miserable waifs soon enough."

At this callous remark, a tart response came to Vi's mind. But looking up at the tall, haughty woman, Vi saw something in Miss Pepper's eyes that stopped her from speaking. Instead of chiding Miss Pepper, Vi said, "Perhaps you would enjoy touring the mission. You didn't have time to see all our facilities when you were here last."

"That would be instructive, I'm sure," Miss Pepper said. "I would be interested in scrutinizing your kitchen. I happen to be a devoted student of nutrition and scientific homemaking. It is so important for the poor among us to learn to feed themselves in a healthful and energizing manner," Miss Pepper continued, "and to organize their kitchens for the utmost efficiency. If I could speak to your cook. . ."

She interrupted herself when she caught sight of an approaching figure.

From behind Vi, a warmly gracious voice said, "Penelope Pepper! My dear, you are the last person I expected to see here."

A thin smile broke on Miss Pepper's face. "Mrs. Travilla, how pleasant to encounter you today," Penny Pepper replied in a tone almost, Vi thought, of relief.

"Miss Pepper has volunteered to help with the new day nursery," Vi told her mother. "I was just proposing to give her a tour. She has expressed a special interest in seeing the kitchen and meeting Mary."

"But darling, you haven't eaten yet," Elsie said to Vi. "I have finished, so I would be delighted to be Penelope's tour guide."

"That would be very pleasant," Miss Pepper agreed.

Elsie took the uninvited guest gently by the arm and guided her toward the house. Vi sent a short, silent prayer of gratitude heavenward. *Thank You, Dear Lord, for my wonderful, sensitive, understanding mother. I know You sent Penny Pepper to us today. I don't know why, but I trust Your reasons. Please, Lord, just help me to hold my tongue and give me a little of my mother's patience for the next few hours.*

"Who's that lady?" Lulu asked when Vi sat down.

"That's Penelope Pepper," Rosemary blurted out before Vi could answer. "Her papa owns the Pepper cotton mills and a bunch of warehouses, and a bank, too."

"Pepper?" said one of the neighborhood girls. "My mamma's a night cleaner at his bank."

"My pa works for old man Pepper at the warehouses," said another girl. "Daddy says Mr. Pepper works his people like mules and pays 'em peanuts."

"Peanuts!" the first girl laughed. "That's a good one. Guess he saves the real money to spend on his girl's feathered hats."

Several other comments were made about Mr. Pepper and his stinginess, until Vi commented, "What you all say may be true, but should we blame Miss Pepper?"

The girls fell silent for some seconds. Then one of them said, "Naw, it ain't her fault. I guess if my father was rich, I'd be showing off my hoity-toity clothes and feathers. But what's she doing here, I wonder?"

Violet's Defiant Daughter

All the girls looked at Vi. Laying down her fork, Vi said, "Miss Pepper is going to assist with the new day nursery. She came today to offer her help with our party."

"Help!" whooped one of the girls in laughter. "I can't exactly picture Miss Pepper up to her elbows in dishwater. You didn't see it, Miss Vi, but when she went into the house, she didn't even look at us. Your ma smiled so pretty and said such nice words to us, but not Miss high-and-mighty Pepper. Passed us by like we're no more than dust balls in a dirty corner."

Vi knew she had to bring such conversation to a halt, but at the same time, she understood the resentment in the girls' words. Gently she said, "Jesus tells us to turn the other cheek. It's important that we not make harsh judgments about people we don't know. You girls understand what motives are—the reasons why we do certain things. Let's say that someone passes you without speaking to you"—Vi was careful not to use Miss Pepper's name—"and you think the person is being mean or snobbish. But could there be other reasons for the slight?"

The girls looked at one another, considering the possibilities. Then Megan Mooney, a gentle girl of about Rosemary Travilla's age, said, "Maybe the person didn't see me. Or maybe she had troubles on her mind and was givin' all her thoughts to them."

"Some folks are just real shy about speaking up," an older girl said.

"Or the person might be feeling poorly," suggested Megan, who, Vi remembered, had a job in a shirt factory. "When I sew all day long, working over those tiny stitches gives me such a headache that I could walk by my own dear mother and not see her."

"So what you're getting' at, Miss Vi," remarked Tilda Nedley, the girl who had laughed at Miss Pepper, "is that we can't always know why people do what they do."

"Sometimes we may know a person's motives," Vi replied thoughtfully. "But often we don't. I've always had a bad tendency to leap to conclusions. Hardly a day goes past that I don't ask the Lord to help me be patient, seek understanding, and not make hasty judgments."

"Jesus says that in the Good Book, 'bout not judging others," said Megan. "But I can't remember the words exactly."

Vi smiled at the young seamstress. "Maybe you mean what He tells us in Matthew 7:1-2. 'Do not judge, or you too will be judged. For in the same way you judge others, you will be judged, and with the measure you use, it will be measured to you.'"

Tilda Nedley shook her head slowly from side to side and said, "Guess I oughta heed what He says and not be so hard on that Miss Pepper. Guess I oughta ask Him for more patience, like you do, Miss Vi." Then Tilda looked around at the other girls, and in a jolly tone, she said, "We ain't hardly let Miss Vi eat, and we're all done. Let's take our plates to the kitchen. Maybe we can help with the washin' up."

With much bustling, the other girls hurried inside. Lulu, however, lingered on the porch with Vi.

"I like the way you do that, Miss Vi," Lulu said.

"Do what, Lulu?" Vi asked. She popped a piece of cornbread into her mouth.

"The way you teach lessons without really seeming like you're teaching. You could have gotten mad at the way the girls were talking about that lady. You could have made a big speech and had everybody feeling guilty and bad. That's what my Aunt Gert used to do. I'd do something she didn't like, and even if it wasn't something naughty, she'd talk and talk at me, telling me I was the worst little girl in the whole world."

"You don't think that of yourself, do you, Lulu?" Vi asked.

"Not always," Lulu replied softly, "but sometimes I do."

"Well, you're not the worst little girl, and I don't want you to think that way anymore," Vi said with conviction. "As a matter of fact, you are dearly loved by your Heavenly Father. So loved that His Son sacrificed His life for you. And if you love the Lord with all your heart, He will always forgive you and help you with your struggles. Do you think He thinks you are truly the worst little girl in the world?"

"I guess not," Lulu said. Then a notion came to her that brought a smile to her lips. "I'd have to be really, really awfully bad all the time to be the *worst* girl. I'd never even have time to sleep. Aunt Gert never thought of that."

"There's something you can do that will please the Lord and make you feel good about yourself," Vi said. She laid her plate aside and took Lulu's hand. "If you pray to Jesus and seek His guidance, He will help you look into your heart and forgive your aunt for her unkind words to you. When we forgive someone—even when they haven't asked for our forgiveness—the Lord washes away our anger and hurt feelings and fills our hearts with the lightness of His love. Will you do that, Lulu? Will you ask the Lord to help you find it in your heart to forgive your aunt, even though it is hard to do?"

"I'll try, Miss Vi," Lulu replied earnestly. "I really will try."

"And I have faith you will succeed," Vi said assuredly. She bent forward and kissed Lulu lightly on the cheek, saying, "I have great faith in the goodness of your heart and the power of God's love, Miss Lulu Raymond."

Then Vi stood and said, "Let me take your plate to the kitchen, while you go and tell Mrs. O'Flaherty that it's time to gather her young singers. We should start our Fourth of July entertainment within the half hour."

⁓

Going to the kitchen, Vi expected to walk in on a scene of laughing, chattering girls helping Mary Appleton with the dishwashing. The sight that greeted her was anything but happy. With heads down, the girls stood as still and silent as statues about the room. Mary was standing as well, but her head was not bowed. Her eyes were dark and stormy, her hands were planted firmly on her hips, and her whole frame was shaking.

The cause of this disturbing tableau was immediately obvious. Miss Penny Pepper was rummaging through the kitchen cabinets and removing items. She was so busy criticizing the arrangement of Mary's domain that she didn't hear Vi enter.

Vi loudly cleared her throat and said, "Is something amiss here?"

Miss Pepper turned on her heel and declared, "Amiss? I should say so, Violet. Your cook apparently has no knowledge of the science of household organization."

Violet heard Mary's angry intake of breath.

"This *lady*," Mary said with heavy sarcasm, "she *says* I'm risking the health of everybody at the mission by keeping my iron pots in that there cabinet. Says they can fall out and kill somebody."

Violet's Defiant Daughter

"A place for everything, and everything in its place," Miss Pepper warbled in a vain attempt to sound light-hearted. "I recently organized my mother's kitchen following the highest principles of household management, and our cook says the change is *unbelievable*."

"I'm quite sure that it is hard to believe," Vi responded in what she hoped was a calm tone. "We will be interested in hearing your ideas, at the appropriate time."

Mary emitted a noisy, huffing sound, and a few titters came from the girls.

"But I'm afraid today is not the best day for cookery lessons," Vi went on. "Mrs. Appleton has a great deal of work to do."

"There's no time like the present," Miss Pepper maintained.

"Quite true," Vi said, "but you are also our guest, and I've come to invite you to join me for our musical program."

"I came to help, not be entertained," Miss Pepper said, holding her ground.

"And we are very grateful," Vi said. "Now that I know of your interest in household science—"

"More than an interest, Violet," Miss Pepper broke in. "Spreading knowledge of this new science is my *cause*."

A fresh wave of titters and giggles arose from the girls.

"And we shall certainly benefit from your knowledge," Vi began again, "if you will—"

She was interrupted, this time by a male voice calling "Hello" from the direction of the back door. Ed Travilla entered and strode across the room to Miss Pepper.

"Miss Penelope," he greeted her in the friendliest fashion. "Mamma told me you were here. She hopes you will sit with us for the songs and music. The children will surely be inspired to do their best with such a fashionable lady in the audience. I hope you will do me the honor of allowing me to escort you to your seat."

Vi put her hand tightly over her mouth to stop a laugh. Ed's exaggerated display of chivalry was accomplishing what she could not hope to achieve by being reasonable. He held out his arm, and the completely entranced Miss Pepper took it. Without another word, she left the kitchen—her hand on Ed's arm and her feathers waving.

A few moments passed in silence; then everyone burst out laughing, even Mary.

"I've never seen you angry before," Vi told her dear friend.

"It's rare, Miss Vi," Mary said, "but that Pepper woman—well—if you hadn't come in when you did—well—I can't say what I'd 'a done to chase her off. Your mamma tried to get her out of here, but she didn't have no more luck than you. I wondered where Miz Travilla went to." Then Mary grinned: "Your mamma's right clever, isn't she. Got that handsome brother of yours to do what we couldn't."

"Mamma is quite perceptive," Vi agreed with a grin that matched Mary's.

Surveying the kitchen, Vi went on, "Everything seems in order, so take off your aprons, ladies. Mrs. O's concert is about to start."

A couple of the girls, who were singing in the chorus, hurried out behind Vi. Rosemary and the others stayed to help Mary with a few last-minute chores.

"Miss Vi's brother rescued us from a terrible fate," laughed Tilda Nedley.

"He's my brother too," Rosemary piped up proudly.

Violet's Defiant Daughter

"Why that's so, ain't it?" Tilda said. "I plum forgot about you being Miss Vi's sister. You've been just one of us girl-friends today, Rosemary — er — Miss Rosemary."

"Oh, please, Tilda, it's only 'Rosemary.'"

Looking into the younger girl's face with kindness, Tilda said, "Well, that's nice of you. You and Miss Vi don't look so similar, but I guess you're a lot alike in more impor-tant ways, what with you both thinking that one person's no better than any other."

Rosemary's plump cheeks glowed with pleasure as she followed Tilda and the other girls outside. In all her life, Rosemary thought, she'd never had such a fine compliment as the one just paid her by Tilda Nedley.

Mrs. O'Flaherty's upright piano had been pushed onto the mission's front porch, and she sat before it on a revolv-ing stool. The members of her chorus, who ranged in age from eight to eighteen, stood in neat rows, the tallest on the porch itself and the younger children — Polly among them — on the steps. People sat in chairs and on folded blan-kets laid over the graveled driveway. The sun had moved below the level of the tall trees, shading the drive. Still, many people cooled themselves with paper fans. Vi took her seat next to Alma Hansen on a blanket. The audience hushed, until the only sound was the soft swishing of the fans.

Mrs. O'Flaherty struck a light chord, and a lanky lad stepped forward, playing "Yankee Doodle" on a wooden flute. He completed a solo round, and then the young voices were raised. By the end of the sprightly song, everyone,

young and old, was either singing the familiar lyrics or clapping to the rousing beat.

Next, Mrs. O'Flaherty led her choristers in the stately "Hail Columbia, Happy Land"—a song first played for the inauguration of President George Washington in 1789. This was followed by very lively, and not always quite on key, renditions of "Oh, Susannah" and "Polly Wolly Doodle."

Mrs. O rose from the piano and spoke to the listeners. "Our next song is a hymn that many of you know—'Eternal Father, Strong to Save.' I have learned that it is traditionally sung at services in the chapel of the Naval Academy at Annapolis. We selected it for our program to honor all who, in peace and war, sail from the seaport of India Bay and those brave citizens of Wildwood who man the docks of our city."

Whispered words of surprise and pleasure rippled through the audience. The hymn was indeed well known, but never before had the people heard it dedicated to the city's dockworkers, so many of whom were residents of Wildwood.

Mrs. O'Flaherty resumed her seat at the piano and hit a note. In perfect unison, the singers began:

Eternal Father, strong to save,
Whose arm hath bound the restless wave,
Who biddest the mighty ocean deep
Its own appointed limits keep,
Oh, hear us when we cry to Thee,
For those in peril in the sea.

Vi marveled at how beautifully the chorus sang and how powerful the emotional response was to their strong young

voices. She'd often heard them practicing over the past weeks, but she hadn't expected such a performance as this. Glancing right and left, she saw the effect on the listeners. Many of the mission's guests had lost loved ones and friends to accidents at sea, on the wharfs, and in the great storms that sometimes battered their coastal homes. A few people applauded softly when the hymn was concluded, but most maintained a reverential silence. Vi thought, *A hymn is a prayer, and this one has touched their hearts and strengthened their hopes.*

Vi looked back at the children and saw that the young seamstress, Megan Mooney, now stood in front of the others. In a voice of astonishing clarity, she sang without accompaniment:

> My country 'tis of Thee,
> Sweet Land of Liberty
> Of thee I sing;
> Land where my fathers died,
> Land of the pilgrims' pride,
> From every mountain side
> Let Freedom ring.

The other girls added their voices to the next verse, and then the boys joined in for two more verses. In spite of the lingering heat, Vi felt goose bumps on her arms. A hand touched hers. It was Alma, who had overcome so much hardship since her arrival from Germany barely six months earlier. "It is a good place," Alma said softly, "this United States of America."

As the final words of "America" died away, the boy with the flute again blew the notes of "Yankee Doodle." Another older boy joined in on a harmonica, and the children took up the song. Each of them raised an arm and began waving a flag—the very paper Stars and Stripes that the Raymond children and Polly had so carefully colored. With the piper leading, the singers marched down the porch steps, formed a line across the front of the mission house, and continued to march in place. When the song ended, Mrs. O hit a single note, and on cue, the children bowed. They were rewarded by a roar of hurrahs, applause, and sharp whistling. Not sure exactly what to do next, some of the younger children bowed again. More clapping and whistling. Now all the children bowed, and still the clapping continued. Mrs. O'Flaherty hurried down the front steps and raised her arms. It took almost a minute for her to make herself heard.

"Thank you, thank you so much," she said with happy laughter. "I am so glad you enjoyed our Fourth of July performance. It was our first, and it will not be our last. You can take great pride in these marvelous young people of Wildwood. You just heard how talented they are. I have been privileged to see how dedicated they are to the hard work of practicing. I feel so, so—"

Mrs. O'Flaherty's strong voice cracked, and Vi thought her friend might be too overcome with emotion to go on. But Mrs. O recovered almost immediately and proclaimed, "I feel so *hungry* for blueberry pie! Dessert is served!"

After a last round of applause, the guests proceeded to the tables where Christine, Kaki, and Miss Moran were handing out plates of fruit pie. Vi looked around, wondering whether she should help Christine or check with Enoch and Mr. Hogg or—

Her thoughts were broken by the approach of her brother. Little Gracie was riding on Ed's broad shoulders. "Whoa, horsie!" Gracie shouted gaily as they came to Vi's side.

Violet's Defiant Daughter

"We've come on a mission from Mamma," Ed said. "She needs help."

"Penny?"

"What else?" Ed laughed. "She is a, shall we say, *determined* woman when it comes to her cause. I doubt that there's an engineer who knows as much about household ventilation and the correct installation of plumbing pipes as she. I've done my duty, little sister. It's your turn now."

"Where are Max and Lulu?" Vi asked.

"Elwood's teaching Max how to throw horseshoes," Gracie said.

"And Lulu went to play with Rosemary and that remarkable young singer," Ed said. "What a beautiful voice that girl has. Perhaps Mrs. O has found a prodigy. Gracie and I are going to find young Polly and enjoy some of Kaki's delicious peach pie."

"Berry for me!" Gracie called out as Ed strode away toward the picnic tables.

Did Ed say "plumbing pipes"? Vi asked herself as she scanned the area and spotted her mother. *What on earth would Penelope Pepper know about plumbing?*

CHAPTER

6

An Explosive Mistake

*An evil man is trapped by
his sinful talk, but a
righteous man escapes
trouble.*

PROVERBS 12:13

An Explosive Mistake

As the afternoon progressed toward sunset, the mission's guests settled into a mood of comradely relaxation. In chairs and on blankets about the lawn, groups of friends chatted quietly. Babies crawled on the grass, and toddlers, tired by play, nestled their heads in their mothers' laps. The elderly checkers players in the backyard continued their games, determined to do battle until the last ray of light ended their competitions. At the horseshoe pitch, Enoch and Mr. Hogg, with Dr. Bowman now on their side, were finally getting in their challenge game against the three Hogg brothers, who had evened the odds by recruiting Ed Travilla. Max and Danny were tossing a baseball with a group of local boys, who argued amicably about whether India Bay would ever have a professional baseball team like the Brooklyn Trolley Dodgers, the Boston Beaneaters, or the Baltimore Orioles.

Lulu, Rosemary, and Megan Mooney were playing a game of jacks on the front porch when Vi walked out the front door. "Play with us," Rosemary invited.

"I wish I could, but I have to tell everyone about the watermelons," Vi replied.

At the girls' questioning looks, she explained, "Our brother sent a cartload of ripe melons from Ion yesterday. We put them in the storage shed, and I almost forgot about them."

"I see you've escaped from Miss Pepper," Rosemary said with a smirk.

"Don't be rude, little sister," Vi said with mock sternness. "Miss Pepper is with Emily Clayton in the clinic. I'm sure they're having a fascinating conversation about hygiene and such matters."

"Poor Miss Clayton," Rosemary said under her breath.

"Can we do something to help you, Miss Vi?" Lulu asked.

"Later perhaps," Vi smiled. "Just enjoy yourselves for now. Oh, but do tell everyone you see about the watermelons. The shed is open, and there should be enough for every family."

Vi left, and the girls continued their game for quite a while, until Rosemary suggested they look for the other girls. But Lulu said she wanted to go to the back garden and watch the horseshoe games. Parting from her friends, Lulu followed the driveway along the street side of the mission grounds. She wasn't in a hurry. She was thinking about the girls she'd met that day. They were all older than she, but they had welcomed her into their group. She'd been surprised to learn that none of the Wildwood girls went to school. Most of them, like Megan, had factory or mill jobs, and when they talked about their work and the long hours of labor, it sounded very difficult. A couple of the older girls were housemaids in wealthy India Bay homes, and they told amusing stories about their employers. Lulu had many questions she wanted to ask, but she kept her queries to herself. For such a curious person, Lulu felt shy about prying into the lives of these hard-working girls.

She was so involved in her thoughts that she didn't notice some boys huddled behind an azalea bush just beside the steps that rose to the small back porch of the house.

"Hey, girlie," a boy said, as she neared the bush.

She looked around for the source of the voice.

"Yeah, you," the boy said in a rough whisper. "Wanna see something funny?"

She went to the leafy bush and saw three boys about her age hunkered on the ground. They had dirty faces and shabby clothes, and one of them was grinning at her. He grabbed her wrist and pulled her down.

"Gotta stay outta sight of the grown folks," said the boy who pulled at her.

Dropping to her knees, Lulu asked, "What are you doing?"

"Just something funny," the boy said. "You stay here, girlie, and keep quiet. It's gonna be a good joke. Really good, I can tell ya."

The other two boys had turned their backs to Lulu, and they seemed to be working over something, but she couldn't see what it was. *Maybe they're playing marbles or jackstraws,* she thought.

"What do you have there?" she asked.

"Just something," said the grinning boy. "You'll see soon enough. Now, it ain't nothin' bad. Just hush up and watch."

Lulu knew that she should leave, but her curiosity, which she'd kept in check all day, finally got the best of her. She tried to see what the boys were doing, but the bush, thick with small, glossy leaves on spiky branches, obscured her view. The boy had said they weren't doing anything bad, and Lulu decided to believe him. A minute went by, and another. The boys were whispering, but Lulu couldn't make out their words. From above the hiding place, she heard a door opening and the clatter of boots on the wooden planks of the porch. The feet stopped, and a woman spoke, but the voice was muffled. Lulu began to feel nervous. She wanted to jump up and get away, but she didn't move.

In an excited way, the grinning boy hissed, "Light it!"

Lulu heard a scratching noise, and one of the boys pushed the azalea branches aside and darted out to set something on the middle porch step. Through the opening the boy made, Lulu could finally see the object. It looked like a large, green ball. *What's funny about that?* Lulu thought. Then she saw some tiny sparks of light that seemed to be climbing the side of the ball.

The clatter of footsteps above her resumed. The woman was coming down the steps! Instantly, Lulu realized what was about to happen. She tried to stand up and shout a warning, but the boys were scrambling away, and one of them pushed her hard. Lulu fell backward into the bush, and her voice caught in her throat.

Before she could get her breath and yell out, a loud bang hit her ears, followed by an even louder scream and a heavy thump. Shouts went up from the old men at the checker tables, and more men began shouting and running toward the house.

Lulu struggled to get up, but the skirt of her dress had become twisted in the azalea branches. By the time she untangled herself, a group of men and boys were gathered around the back steps. Lulu stood and saw Miss Pepper in her silver gray dress sitting oddly on the bottom step. The woman's eyes were shut, and she wasn't moving, but something red and watery was running down her face and over the bodice of her dress. The red stuff even dripped from the feathers of her hat.

"Just look at that blood!" an old man was shouting. "Poor woman got her brains blowed out!"

An Explosive Mistake

"No, no!" came the voice of Dr. Bowman, who bent over Miss Penny Pepper. Lulu saw the doctor touch Miss Pepper's wet, red brow and then put his fingers to his lips. "It's watermelon pulp, not blood!"

Emily Clayton hurried down the porch steps, and she handed a little bottle to Dr. Bowman. He uncorked the smelling salts and waved the bottle under Miss Pepper's nose. The lady came to with a start, and the doctor instructed her not to move until he checked for any broken bones. With her usual efficiency, Emily directed the small crowd back from the stairs. The men and boys lingered for a minute, but hearing from the doctor that the lady was not dead or even injured, they soon dispersed out of consideration for her privacy. Only Ed Travilla stayed to assist.

Christine and Kaki had come from the kitchen at the sound of the explosion and Miss Pepper's shriek. The doctor and Ed lifted Miss Pepper to her feet, and Kaki gently wiped the sticky red pulp from her face with a towel.

Miss Pepper recovered her voice much quicker than her dignity. In piercing tones, she demanded, "Who did this to me? Who is responsible? I must know who did this cruel thing! Someone call the police! I want the villainous miscreant jailed for assault! Whoever did this must be made to pay! My father will see that I am avenged!"

Vi, her mother, and Mrs. O'Flaherty arrived in the middle of Miss Pepper's tirade, and Elsie Travilla immediately took over, soothing the trembling lady and encouraging her to come inside and lie down. Penny Pepper went without argument, but she didn't halt her steady stream of demands: "Summon the constabulary! Tell them to bring leg irons! These awful people must be put in their place!"

Violet's Defiant Daughter

When the kitchen door closed, Vi, Ed, and Mrs. O'Flaherty looked at Dr. Bowman. "It was a prank," he said, pointing at the shattered remains of the watermelon on the step.

"Someone threw a watermelon at her?" Mrs. O asked in disbelief.

"Not *threw*," said the doctor. He knelt down, looking for something under the azalea. After a few moments, he rose and displayed a short piece of blackened string, some tiny bits of soggy paper, and a small wet cylinder with a wick. "Someone put firecrackers in the watermelon and lit the fuse. This cracker was too soaked with melon juice to go off. It's a boys' trick—weave all the cracker wicks together and light them with a single fuse to create a bigger bang. I'm sure the rascals who played this joke had no intent to harm."

"I wonder where they got the firecrackers," Vi said.

"They're easy enough to find, and usually poorly made," the doctor said. "Even a poor boy can get them, if he has a few pennies. Whoever made this little bomb packed the melon full. The fruit absorbed most of the blast, so Miss Pepper was showered with pulp, not hard pieces of rind. She merely fainted from surprise."

Lulu had not stirred through all the confusion, and no one seemed to notice her where she stood, behind the azalea bush. She'd been terribly frightened, and her legs still felt weak. Even though she was an innocent bystander, she felt guilty about what had happened, and she was very glad that Miss Pepper was not hurt.

Ed was just saying that he supposed they should find the boys who played the prank when a rough hand took hold of Lulu's arm and jerked her forward.

An Explosive Mistake

"Here's one of yer criminals," said a short, red-faced young man in a dark woolen jacket. He was Miss Pepper's driver, and away from his bossy mistress, he was no longer the meek servant Vi had met earlier in the afternoon.

"I saw her hiding in that bush just before the bang," the man went on. "Some boys were running away like their tails were on fire, but this little missy got herself hung on them branches. No doubt she can tell you who them young thugs are. These Wildwood kids all stick together like thieves."

Vi, Ed, Mrs. O, and the doctor were all staring at Lulu in utter amazement. Her pretty white dress was streaked with dirt, her sash was undone, and the lace trim from one of her sleeves dangled against her arm. Her hair, tangled with twigs and leaves, tumbled from her braid, and her pretty hair ribbon was nowhere to be seen. There were thin red whelps on her arms, and a long, bloody scratch ran down one cheek to her jawline.

"What has happened to you, Lulu?" Vi exclaimed, taking the girl in her arms.

"She's done got caught red-handed," the short driver said. "Guilty as sin, she is. Miss Pepper's gonna be mighty pleased with me for nabbing this brat. Might even make me her full-time driver."

Ignoring the puffed-up driver, Vi said, "Did you see what happened, Lulu?"

"Yes, Miss Vi," Lulu said in a shaky whisper. "But I don't know the boys who did it."

"Lying little minx," the driver spat out harshly. "She knows 'em. She might be their leader, like them female pirates you hear stories about."

"I didn't!" Lulu cried. "I didn't do it. Those boys said— they said—"

Violet's Defiant Daughter

Lulu burst into tears, the salty flood from her eyes stinging the cut on her face.

"Be quiet, man," Ed demanded of the driver. "You didn't see enough of what occurred to lay blame on this child."

"But *I* saw what happened," said a clear voice with a strong European accent.

Everyone except Lulu, whose face was buried against Vi's skirt, looked up to see a young man in a leather jacket. He was tall, but his wide-brimmed, Western-style hat cast his face in shadow.

"I did not anticipate the exploding watermelon," he said evenly. "If I had, I would have stopped those young fellows. I was standing on the other side of the driveway, and I saw three boys, maybe ten or eleven years old, get the melon from that building"—he gestured at the shed—"and bring it here. I guessed they were going to eat it. It was some time before this young girl walked by. One of the boys grabbed her hand and pulled her to her knees. He talked to her, but I could not overhear his words. I assumed she was a sister of the lad and thought nothing of it. This girl never moved, and I do not think she could see anything. It could not have been more than two minutes before I saw the boys racing from beneath the bush. One of them knocked the girl into the bush. Then the blast came. This young girl got to her feet and stood there until this man"—he nodded at the flustered driver—"dragged her away so roughly. Please forgive me, ladies and sirs, but I listened to what he said, and he does not truly know what happened. He came running here after the explosion."

"Thank you," Mrs. O'Flaherty said. Then getting directly to the point, she asked, "Who are you?"

An Explosive Mistake

The young man doffed his hat, revealing curly auburn hair, a sunbaked countenance, and hazel eyes that were red-rimmed with fatigue.

"Forgive my poor manners," he said with a gentle smile that seemed familiar to Vi. "I have traveled a long way to reach this place, and I'm not at my best. My intention was to introduce myself after your party was ended, for I do not like to intrude myself. My name is Rudy Hansen, and if God has directed me aright, I believe you ladies must be Mrs. O'Flaherty and Miss Travilla."

"Alma's brother!" Mrs. O'Flaherty exclaimed. "Oh, my boy, our gracious God has indeed directed you to the right place!"

"We must find Alma!" Vi declared. "*Herr* Hansen, how she has longed for this day. But we thought you were coming at the end of the month."

"I became too impatient," Rudy said, "for the sight of my beloved sister. I left San Francisco almost two weeks ago."

"You wait here, and I will get Alma," Mrs. O'Flaherty said, turning to go.

"Tell her what to expect," Dr. Bowman called after Mrs. O. "One lady in a faint is my limit for today."

Standing at the edge of this scene, Miss Pepper's carriage driver could only shake his head in frustration. His hopes of playing the hero for his employer's daughter, and perhaps earning a promotion for himself, had been dashed. Having lost his chance for glory, he could only slip away and sulk.

Meanwhile, Rudy Hansen was saying, "This little girl is innocent. I suspect the boys pushed her to the ground in order that she would be left behind to take the blame. In the excitement, she might have run away. To her credit, she stayed."

Lulu could not believe this sudden turn of events. She hadn't prayed for help—she'd been too scared—*but God must have been watching over me the whole time,* she thought, *protecting me. I never could have defended myself against that other man! God sent this Western man to help me.* There was no other way to explain how he had come to Samaritan House on this day and had been in just the right place to see what happened and rescue her. It couldn't be a coincidence. *Miss Vi told me how much God loves me,* Lulu remembered. For the first time, Lulu thought that maybe it could be true.

Lulu didn't see the reunion between Alma Hansen and her brother. Dr. Bowman had insisted that she go with him to the clinic, so he could treat the cut on her face. "I think you have your own knight in shining armor," he said, as he washed the cut and dabbed on an antiseptic.

"I think God sent Mr. Hansen," Lulu said.

"I believe He did," the kindly physician responded. "As it says in Psalm 46, 'God is our refuge and strength, an ever-present help in trouble.'"

"I hope Miss Pepper is okay," Lulu said. "I tried to warn her, but that boy knocked me over, and I couldn't get the words out in time."

"Miss Pepper suffered no worse than watermelon stains to her fashionable gown and some pain to her pride," Dr. Bowman said. "God was watching over her, too. There now, Lulu. The cut isn't deep, but you must keep it very clean until it begins to heal well. We don't want any infection."

"I'll keep it clean, I promise," Lulu said. "May I go outside now?"

An Explosive Mistake

"It's getting dark, I'm afraid, so our friends may be inside. Go along and find them. I'll be down in a few minutes," the doctor said, dismissing his young patient with a fatherly pat on her shoulder.

───────◦───────

Miss Pepper had departed by the time Lulu came down from the clinic, and so had the rest of the day's guests, including the Travilla family. Lulu saw no one in the mission's meeting room, but she heard music and followed the melodic sounds out to the porch, where Mrs. O'Flaherty was sitting at the piano and singing.

On a little wicker settee, Gracie was sitting in Vi's lap, and Christine was in a chair next to them, with little Jacob asleep in her arms. Emily Clayton was in another chair, holding Polly. Miss Moran and Kaki were there, too, and Mary, who had labored harder than anyone on a day of challenging work, had the place of honor on a chaise lounge. Max was leaning against the porch railing, and there was just enough light for Lulu to see Enoch and Elwood Hogg in the driveway.

Vi motioned to Lulu, and the girl slipped into the space next to her on the settee.

Gracie saw the cut on her sister's face and asked, "Are you hurt bad, Lulu?"

"It's just a scratch," Lulu said. "Doctor Bowman fixed it for me."

Max also noticed his sister's face. He came over, examined her, and asked, "How'd that happen?"

"It's a good story, but can I tell you tomorrow, Max?" Lulu replied. "I'm kind of tired all of a sudden."

Violet's Defiant Daughter

Vi slipped her arm around Lulu's shoulders, and Lulu sank comfortably against Vi's side. "It was a really good party, Miss Vi," Lulu said.

"Thank you, darling," Vi said. She leaned over and whispered in Lulu's ear, "You will have a very good story to tell, since no one was hurt. Your Papa would like to hear it, too. You could write about the exploding watermelon in your next letter to him."

Lulu nodded. *"The Remarkable Adventure of the Exploding Watermelon,"* she thought. *It sounds like a real story in a magazine. And it has a real hero too!*

She sat up and asked, "Where's Mr. Hansen? I need to thank him."

"He's upstairs," Vi said. "Alma is helping him unpack, for he will be staying here at the mission. Don't worry. You'll have many opportunities to thank him."

Lulu settled back against Vi and closed her eyes. Mrs. O'Flaherty was singing one of the beautiful ballads of Stephen Foster, and the gentle lyrics and melody washed soothingly over Lulu.

"I've got to thank God, too," she said sleepily. "He sent Mr. Hansen to rescue me. I have to make a prayer and tell Him how good He is to me. And how much I. . ."

Lulu's voice faded, and Vi felt the young body relax under her arm.

"You have already made your prayer, my dearest," Vi whispered to the sleeping girl, "and our Heavenly Father has heard every word in your heart."

CHAPTER

Exciting News

*A cheerful look brings joy
to the heart, and good
news gives health to
the bones.*

PROVERBS 15:30

Exciting News

fter the Fourth of July picnic, Lulu finally decided that Miss Vi really was a friend. What settled her mind was the way Vi had acted about the watermelon prank. *If Aunt Gert had been there*, Lulu told herself, *she'd have blamed me no matter what anybody said. That's what she always did in Boston — blamed Max and me for anything that went wrong. Aunt Gert would have lectured me and told me that I'm so bad that nobody would ever love me.*

On Sunday, after attending their church service and enjoying one of Miss Moran's good lunches, Lulu retreated to her hidey hole in the boxwood bushes, where she could be alone with her thoughts. *I guess Miss Vi could have blamed me, since I'd played that dumb joke with the frogs. But Miss Vi didn't think I did it, even when that driver man was saying I did. I hope I never see that man again!*

Lulu lay down on the soft straw and rested her head on an old pillow she'd brought from the house. She looked up into the low, green canopy overhead, and said aloud, "I guess that I really like Miss Vi. I guess that I want her to be my friend."

Inside her, a voice of doubt seemed to say, *But she wants to be your stepmother, doesn't she? She wants to marry your Papa and make him forget about your own sweet mother. If you trust her, she'll wreck your family. That's what stepmothers do, isn't it?*

Lulu was beginning to be very annoyed by that quarrelsome, nagging voice that always wanted her to doubt herself. "She *doesn't* want to be my stepmother," Lulu argued back defiantly. "Miss Vi loves the mission, and she'd *never* leave the people in Wildwood. I bet she never gets married to anybody, so you're all wrong. I have a right to change my mind, and I can be Miss Vi's friend if I want to be!"

Her doubts retreated, and Lulu smiled to herself. "Miss Vi is my friend. And so are Mrs. O'Flaherty and the people at Samaritan House and Miss Vi's family. And Miss Moran and Kaki. It feels good to have friends."

Her doubt came back: *Don't trust. . .* But Lulu cut it off and filled her mind with thoughts about the coming week. Miss Vi would be taking her and Gracie to see their new school, and Mrs. O'Flaherty had promised the girls a trip to the public library. Ed and Danny Travilla were coming to the city to take Max to visit his school, and then Max was going to stay at Ion for a few days. Lulu didn't begrudge her brother's visit to the Travillas' home. She was glad that Max and Danny had become friends. Besides, Miss Zoe Love, who lived with Miss Vi's grandparents, was coming to visit the mission.

Lulu had met Miss Zoe once before and thought her very nice and very beautiful. But recalling that day, when her father had taken them to Ion, brought back the unsettling memory of an overheard conversation and words that seemed to threaten Lulu's happiness. Her doubt tried to speak again, but again Lulu pushed it away. *I liked Miss Zoe a lot. Maybe she'll be our friend too*, Lulu thought hopefully.

Most of all, Lulu was looking forward to a letter from her father. He'd been gone for almost a week. If anyone could end her doubts, it was her father. Surely his letter would come soon.

Exciting News

Lulu and Gracie's visit to their new school came in the middle of the week after the Fourth. Lulu didn't admit it, even to her little sister, but she was very nervous. She had not liked her school in Boston, where the teachers were always cross and stern. Mark had assured her that Miss Broadbent's was a fine school and that Lulu would like it. Even so, Lulu's stomach was full of butterflies on the morning that Vi and Zoe Love came to get Gracie and her. Lulu was glad to see Miss Zoe in the buggy, for it was hard to be worried and unhappy when she was around. Still, Lulu's stomach made a little leap as Vi drove the buggy through a pair of iron gates hung from two large stone pillars. An engraved metal plaque attached to one of the pillars read:

MISS BROADBENT'S FEMALE ACADEMY
Established 1874

This school started the year I was born, Lulu thought as the buggy halted before a large building in the same gray stone as the pillared gates. A nice-looking woman, who appeared to be about her Papa's age, was standing on the front steps. *Maybe she's one of the teachers*, Lulu thought hopefully. *But probably not. She's too young, and she's smiling. My teachers in Boston never smiled like that.*

"Welcome," the woman said in a low, melodious voice. She looked at Lulu and Gracie with clear, bright eyes. "I am Miss Susan Broadbent, and I am so pleased to meet my two new pupils."

Lulu could have been knocked over with a feather. She had expected the headmistress of Miss Broadbent's Female Academy to be old, stiff, and probably ugly. That was the kind of person she'd often read about in stories of children sent to dark and drafty schools where they endured terrible suffering at the hands of heartless and cruel schoolmistresses. Lulu's imagination had not prepared her for the young woman who showed the girls to her office and gave them cookies before taking them on a tour.

Both Vi and Zoe had seen the startled look on Lulu's face when Susan Broadbent introduced herself. "Lulu was expecting a dragon lady," Zoe whispered as she and Vi followed the girls and Miss Broadbent inside. "Does Lulu's imagination frequently play such tricks on her?"

"I believe it may," Vi replied thoughtfully.

The visit went very well. They had a long chat about Gracie's and Lulu's previous schooling and their interests. Miss Broadbent told them about the classes they would be taking, and by the time the visit ended, it was decided that Gracie would enter the first grade and Lulu the fifth grade.

"I am so glad that you both like to read," Miss Broadbent said as she helped the girls into Vi's buggy. "I have given Miss Travilla a list of books, and I hope you will read several during the summer. Choose the ones you want. If you need advice, Miss Travilla and Miss Love will help you."

"What a wonderful place!" Zoe said as they passed through the gates. "I'm sure you're going to enjoy it and be very good scholars."

Gracie began talking with great animation about Miss Broadbent and the school. Lulu sat back in her seat, thinking. *Maybe it won't be so bad. Maybe it won't be bad at all.*

Miss Moran was waiting on the porch when the buggy returned to College Street. Her face was flushed, and she was obviously excited about something.

"It's just come!" she called out. "Your father's letter!"

Exciting News

Lulu and Gracie scrambled out of the buggy's narrow backseat and raced to Miss Moran. "Where's Max?" Lulu asked.

"Playing baseball with his friend Willy," Miss Moran said. "Kaki has gone to fetch him home."

Vi and Zoe had come up to the porch to say good-bye, but Lulu said, "Please stay. You want to hear what Papa has written, don't you?"

Just then Max ran up. "Have you read it yet?" he asked.

"We waited for you," Lulu said. "You're the oldest, and you should read it to us."

Miss Moran handed Max the letter, and the three children sat on the porch steps. The women stood quietly to the side. After wiping his dusty hands on his trousers, Max carefully unsealed the envelope, drew out the pages, and began to read:

My Dearest Gracie, Lulu, and Max,

I will be on the way to Yucatan by the time you read this. I can tell you that I have been working hard and have had little time for sightseeing. Dr. Hockingham, the leader of our expedition, does not let any of us be lazy. He hired mule carts for our journey, and today we finished loading our supplies and equipment. We leave tomorrow before dawn. There are ten of us in addition to Professor Hockingham—myself, three of the professor's students, one of his assistants (Malachi Bottoms, who is our artist), an experienced guide whose name is Miguel Hernandez, and four workers, one of whom is our cook.

Violet's Defiant Daughter

Dr. Hockingham mapped the way to the site on his previous trip, but the tropical forests change quickly, and the map may not be of much use. We are fortunate to have Señor Hernandez to lead us. The site is in an area without much population, so there are no nice towns where we can shop. But we have strong tents to sleep in and plenty of food. Our cook, Luis, assures me that we have more than enough rice and *frijoles* (that's "beans" to you).

If you look at the globe in my library, you'll see that Yucatan is surrounded on three sides by water. We are going to the southern middle part of this Mexican state, so we won't be near the sea. The site we seek is in a heavily forested area, where Dr. Hockingham believes there was a city of the ancient Maya people. We will spend most of our time clearing trees and digging for evidence of the city. When I return, I hope to bring news of an important find. If we don't make the discovery for which we all hope, the work still will have been worthwhile. I am even learning a new language—a fascinating mixture of Spanish and native Indian tongues. I shall teach you what I learn when I see you.

How I look forward to the day when we are together again. You know how much I love my work, but it is nothing compared to my affection for my three wonderful children. I want you all to have a grand summer, your first in the South. Max, how is that throwing arm of yours? You will probably be able to pitch your baseball as straight as an arrow by the end of summer. And Gracie, remember to eat all your vegetables and get plenty of exercise. Are you seeing your friend Polly very often? Perhaps she might stay the night with you sometime. And Lulu, when I mentioned to Mr. Bottoms that my elder daughter is a great reader of adventure books, he was delighted, for he reads adventure with as much pleasure as you do. He suggests you try the books of Mr. Jules Verne, especially *Around the World in Eighty Days*, which he says is a grand story for someone who dreams of travel to distant places.

I have not forgotten my promise to my children. Someday, we shall all see the world together. This trip is a great opportunity for me, but how I wish you were here with me. Each day, when I read my Bible, I feel especially close to you, because I know that you are doing the same and that our Heavenly Father is watching over you and keeping you safe. He has blessed us with Miss Moran and Kaki and Miss Vi and our friends at Samaritan House, and I know that you will be good for them and will turn to them whenever you are in need.

I must end now, for Professor Hockingham has a few more things for us to do before we sleep. Just remember, my precious children, that my heart is there with you always, and I will always be your loving and proud,

Papa

Gracie took the letter and ran her fingers over the pages, touching her father's writing as gently as if she were touching his cheek. No one spoke for some time. Then in her cheerful way, Miss Moran said, "Professor Raymond will have some grand stories for us when he returns. Oh, I do hope they find that ancient city."

"And you three will have much to tell your father on his return," Vi said, adopting Miss Moran's light tone. "Tell me, have you been working on your letters to him?"

"Yes, ma'am," replied Max. "We all have. When do you think we should mail them, Miss Vi? So they'll be there when he gets back to Mexico City."

"I would think that two weeks in advance would be fine," Vi said, "but I will ask our postman if that is adequate."

"Miss Vi," Lulu said, "do you know how I could get that book Papa wrote about? I'd like to read it before he comes home."

Vi smiled and said, "If you don't mind reading a used book, I have a copy of *Around the World in Eighty Days* at the mission. My brother Ed gave it to me years ago, when he went away to college. It's a great adventure, Lulu."

Lulu was regarding Miss Vi with wondering eyes. "You read adventure books?" she asked with interest.

"Oh, yes. Some people think girls shouldn't like tales of adventure, but I've always enjoyed them very much. When I read stories about faraway places, it's as though I'm really there," Vi said, her eyes twinkling. "It will give me pleasure to share an adventure with you, Lulu. And I do believe that Mr. Verne's novel is on Miss Broadbent's summer reading list."

"What list?" Max asked, and the girls began telling him about the visit to their new school.

Vi and Zoe said their good-byes, and Vi said she'd be back the next morning to get Lulu and Gracie for their day at the mission. Vi might have stayed longer, but in truth, she was anxious to return to Wildwood. She hoped that she too might have received a letter that day—a letter from Mexico.

Exciting News

Vi did find a letter waiting for her. Mark had included some of the same information in the children's letter, but mostly he had written of feelings that were for Vi alone and of his hopes and dreams for their future together. Vi read his long letter several times, and as Gracie had done, she ran her fingers over the bold handwriting. There were parts of the letter that she also wanted to share, at least with Mrs. O'Flaherty, but most of it she would keep to herself and cherish in her heart.

That night in her office, Vi set aside her account books and business correspondence to begin her reply to Mark. She wrote for about an hour before deciding to complete her letter the next day. Carefully she stored Mark's letter and her own unfinished one in a small drawer in the desktop and locked it with a little key.

It was late when she went upstairs, but she saw that Mrs. O'Flaherty's light was still burning, and she knocked at her friend's door. Mrs. O'Flaherty was in bed, reading. "Well, how is the Professor?" Mrs. O asked when Vi entered.

"Well and happy," Vi replied. "I will show you his letter tomorrow."

"That isn't necessary, Vi girl," Mrs. O'Flaherty said. "You shared his letters with me in the past, but now you are engaged and soon you will be married. There are communications between couples that are for them alone, so you keep your letters private, my dear. I trust you to tell me what I need to know."

"I am so used to telling you and Mamma everything," Vi said. She sat down on the side of the bed.

"You shall change many habits when you are Mrs. Marcus Raymond," Mrs. O'Flaherty laughed. "I can tell you from experience that it is not so simple at first to think of yourself as *two* people and to consider each decision from your own and your husband's perspectives. Yet even when you and the professor disagree — and you will not always be of the same mind — you will find yourself respecting his feelings as he respects yours."

Mrs. O then shifted her position and said, "On another subject, how long will we have Zoe with us?"

"She had planned on a week, but after our visit with Miss Broadbent today, Zoe said she might stay as long as two weeks," Vi said. "I saw the two of them with their heads together. I don't know what they were discussing, but I think there may be some plan afoot."

"Between Zoe and Susan Broadbent?" Mrs. O'Flaherty asked in surprise. "I should have known that our Zoe would bring a new mystery with her, but it is too late tonight to try to solve it. I am just glad we will have her here for a good, long visit. Now, dear, shall we read our Bibles together? You choose the passage."

Two days later, Max went off for his visit to Ion. But Lulu and Gracie hardly had time to miss him, for they spent their days at the mission. Zoe and Mrs. O'Flaherty took them and Polly on excursions to the library, to a brass band concert in one of the city's parks, and on a very special day, to tea at the home of Dr. and Mrs. Silas Lansing, a prominent couple who were great friends of the Travilla family and of the mission. Vi made time for this last event. She hadn't seen the Lansings for a few weeks and looked forward to telling them about the latest developments at Samaritan House. As it turned out, the mission was the main topic of conversation, but not in the way Vi expected.

There was another guest at the Lansings' when they arrived. Dr. Lansing introduced him as Mr. Thomas Gibbons. Mrs. Lansing took Mrs. O'Flaherty, Zoe, and the girls off to see her gardens. Then Mr. Gibbons got down to business.

"I have fairly recently become a resident of India Bay," the gentleman said, addressing Vi, "and Dr. and Mrs. Lansing have been so kind to befriend me and my family. They have told me of the work you are doing at your mission. I believe that I can help."

"That would be most gracious of you," Vi said sincerely. She naturally assumed that this rather unremarkable, middle-aged businessman wished to make a donation.

"What I am offering is not a financial gift," Mr. Gibbons said, as if he had read her thoughts. He moved forward in his chair, and his eyes brightened. "I am the president of a new kind of company. Coastal Telephonic Communications, Incorporated. Dr. and Mrs. Lansing have informed me that your mission needs what I sell. A telephone, Miss Travilla! That's what I have to offer."

Vi was taken aback. She had longed for telephone service that would link Wildwood to the rest of India Bay — the police station, the firehouse, the hospital. What a blessing it would be. Vi was wary too, for the mission's budget was not sufficient to cover such a large expense.

"We cannot afford —" Vi began, but Mr. Gibbons cut her off.

"There's nothing to afford!" he exclaimed. "It would be free, Miss Travilla, no strings attached, except the wires we would string to your mission, of course."

He chuckled at his little joke, then said, "My company is new here. If Coastal Telephonic can establish the first telephone service in your community, it will help my business. I believe that India Bay will grow southward, through Wildwood. I want to wire Wildwood to get a head start on my competition. To be frank, a telephone in your mission will be good business for me."

Dr. Lansing cleared his throat and said, "Vi, I think I should tell you that Mr. Gibbons is his company's best salesman, but he's more modest about himself. The man I've come to know has a personal commitment to this city and especially to Wildwood. I do not believe that he will abuse your trust."

Vi's inclination was to agree, yet she was always cautious where the welfare of Samaritan House was concerned. So she said, "It is a very generous proposal, Mr. Gibbons, but there are other people I must consult. Can you wait a few days for an answer?"

"Gladly," Mr. Gibbons said, sitting back in his chair. "I brought some documents that explain how the telephone service works and what the installation involves."

"Thank you," Vi said. "I cannot promise that we will accept, but I will have an answer for you very soon."

Mr. Gibbons soon excused himself, for he had to return to his office. Mrs. Lansing, Mrs. O, Zoe, and the girls returned to the parlor, and they all enjoyed a very nice tea. Mr. Gibbons's offer was not discussed again until, as they were leaving, Vi was taken aside by Mrs. Lansing. "I told you I would get a telephone to the mission," Mrs. Lansing said, "but I had no idea how to do it. Then the Lord led Mr. Gibbons to us. You don't have to make the decision now. I only wanted to say that I have learned a good deal about Mr. Gibbons, and Silas and I have confidence in his honesty. His interest in the mission goes well beyond business."

Vi wanted to know more about Mr. Gibbons, but there wasn't time. She'd promised to get the girls back to College Street in time for supper. Polly was having her first overnight visit with Gracie, and when they got to the Raymond house, Vi had a sudden idea. She turned to Lulu and said, "Polly is staying with Gracie tonight. Would you like to come to Samaritan House in exchange? I'd love for you to be our overnight guest."

"Really?" Lulu said. "I'd like to, if Miss Moran says I can."

"I'll get her permission," Vi said, "while you go pack your things."

"Did you see that?" Zoe asked.

They were passing through the business center of India Bay, and Zoe had been paying close attention to the dresses and hats on display in the windows of the most fashionable shops when something else caught her eye.

"Look, there's another one!" Zoe exclaimed. "A circus poster!"

"I see it!" Lulu cried out.

Vi guided the carriage to the curb and stopped. Zoe got out and went to a boarded-up window in a deserted building, where a poster in red and yellow with large black lettering had been pasted. She paused for a few moments and then got back into the carriage. "The circus is coming to town!" she proclaimed with childlike glee. "Oh, we must go. They will be performing on Friday, Saturday, and next Monday at the fairgrounds. There's an afternoon and an evening show each day. Would you like that, Lulu?" Zoe asked.

"I've never even seen one," Lulu said. "They came to Boston sometimes, but Aunt Gert wouldn't take us. She said that circuses and such make children too excited."

"Your Aunt Gert sounds like a real wet blanket," Zoe giggled.

"Well, I think that we will all enjoy a night at the circus," Vi said as she tightened her grip on the reins. "Saturday night perhaps, after the mission meal and devotion. Maybe Dr. Bowman and Mr. Hansen will go as our escorts."

Zoe reached up and tapped Lulu's arm. Lulu turned around. She was wearing one of those glorious grins that crinkled her nose and made her freckles stand out.

The circus was the main topic of conversation that night at supper. Then after the dishes were done, the young women and Lulu joined Mrs. O'Flaherty in the meeting room. Mrs. O had recently received a packet of new sheet music from a friend in New York, and she entertained her friends with her piano playing until the clock struck nine.

"It's time to get you to bed," Vi told Lulu.

"But where, Miss Vi?" Lulu asked. "All your bedrooms are taken."

Lulu had a curious memory for facts. For example, on her first visit to Samaritan House, she had counted all the rooms in the mission, and she remembered that there were five upstairs bedrooms in addition to Mary and Polly's living

quarters on the ground floor. There was Miss Vi's room and Mrs. O'Flaherty's, and Alma had her own room, and now Rudy was in another room. Plus Miss Zoe. Five rooms, five people.

"I thought you could share with me," Vi said. "The last time Rosemary stayed overnight, the house was full, so we put an extra bed in my room for her. It's very comfortable, Lulu. Would that be all right with you?"

This was Lulu's first time ever to spend the night away from home, and in spite of her adventurous nature, she was a little nervous. Not that she expected anything to happen to her in the mission, but still. . . . It might be easier to sleep, she thought, knowing that Miss Vi was there.

Vi and Zoe accompanied Lulu upstairs. After Lulu washed and got into her nightclothes, Vi excused herself for a few minutes. Lulu settled on the small spare bed in Vi's room, and Zoe brushed her hair and arranged it in a loose braid.

Tugging Lulu's braid playfully, Zoe said, "Your hair is so thick and luxurious, and it waves beautifully. You will grow tall, I think, like your father, and with your golden hair piled high on your head, you will be a very elegant young lady."

"I think my hair's like straw," Lulu said. She couldn't imagine being grown up.

"It's not at all like straw," Zoe laughed. "Brush it gently every night, and it won't tangle so much."

Vi returned just then, saying, "I found it! *Around the World in Eighty Days*. I thought we might read a chapter before your prayers, Lulu. Or are you too tired? You've had a busy day."

"I'm not tired, Miss Vi," Lulu said. "I'd like to start the story tonight."

"Me, too," Zoe said. "You read, Vi, and Lulu and I will stay right here on her very nice bed and listen quietly."

When Vi finished the first chapter, Lulu was already so involved in the story that she asked for another. But Vi said it was getting late, and she took up her Bible.

"Since Mr. Verne's story is about travelers, I thought we might read a story Jesus told about another traveler, a kind stranger who encountered a beaten and wounded man on the road."

"The Good Samaritan?" Lulu guessed. Vi nodded, and Lulu said, "I like that one."

Vi read the brief parable, and then Lulu said her prayers. Though her prayer wasn't long, it was becoming easier for her to talk with the Lord. During her years in Boston, Lulu had been taught to think of God as a harsh and distant judge and a fearsome punisher of sin and evil. But since going to live with her father and especially after moving to India Bay, she had been surrounded by kind, good-willed people who spoke of God as their loving, trustworthy, and unfailing Heavenly Father. After the firecracker incident on the Fourth of July, Lulu started to think that they were right and that Jesus might really be a Friend to her. To *her*—Lulu Raymond! As her heart was changing, her prayers changed too. Instead of praying because she was supposed to, she now found herself beginning to share with the Lord all that was in her heart.

This night her prayer was mostly for others—her father, her sister and brother, her new friends. She also remembered to include the ladies who had been so kind to her when the Raymonds were living in Kingstown. But at the end, she said, "Please, Jesus, help me to be an unselfish person like the Samaritan. I'm trying very hard to be good, but I need Your help sometimes. I guess that's all for right now, Jesus. Thank You."

"That was a very good prayer, Lulu," said Zoe. She hugged the little girl and then rose from the small bed. "I know our Lord will answer your prayer."

Vi came and kissed Lulu's forehead softly. "I have to lock up the house now," Vi said. "Zoe will stay with you till I return. Sleep well, dear Lulu, and have sweet dreams."

With a yawn and a sleepy smile, Lulu said, "I hope I dream 'bout the circus."

CHAPTER

8

A Three-Ring Emergency

You will not fear the terror of night. . .

PSALM 91:5

A Three-Ring Emergency

*L*ulu woke with a start. The room was pitch black, and someone was moving around.

Lulu dared to open one eye, but she couldn't see anything. She heard rustling sounds, and she knew that she wasn't dreaming. Then came a loud *Smack!* Something, a book maybe, had been knocked to the floor. She wanted to pull the sheet over her head and disappear, but she was too frightened to move a muscle.

"Lulu?" a soft voice said. "Did I wake you?"

A huge sigh of relief escaped the little girl, and she sat up. "I'm awake, Miss Vi," she said. "Are you okay?"

"Yes, dear," Vi said. She struck a match and lit a lamp. In the low light, Lulu could see that Miss Vi was fully dressed.

"Is it morning?" Lulu asked.

"No, it's a little before three o'clock," Vi replied. "We have something of an emergency. It's nothing dangerous, and no one is hurt. But I must go out for a while, so Miss Alma is coming to stay with you. You can go back to sleep, and I should be here by the time you get up."

"What happened?" Lulu asked, rubbing the sleep from her eyes.

"Miss Alma will tell you," Vi said, as she went to her door. "And I will tell you more in the morning."

Vi opened the door just as Alma, clad in her nightclothes, was about to knock. Vi hurried out, saying to the seamstress, "Please explain to Lulu what has occurred. Then get some sleep, both of you."

Vi vanished, and Lulu could hear her steps as she ran down the hallway. Alma came to sit on Lulu's bed.

Violet's Defiant Daughter

"The mission has some unexpected guests," Alma said in her slow, careful English. "I do not know who they are, but I heard a great banging at the front door and many voices from downstairs. Miss Vi is taking them to the shelter house."

"By herself?" Lulu said with concern. "Is she safe?"

"My brother, Rudy, goes with her. And Mr. Enoch too," Alma replied with a reassuring smile. "You must sleep now, and we will learn more tomorrow."

Lulu didn't think she could sleep, not with such curious things going on. But she closed her eyes anyway, and she felt Miss Alma's hand gently stroking her forehead. Very softly, Alma sang a song in German. Lulu couldn't understand the words, but Alma's voice was very soothing, and within a few minutes, Lulu was asleep again.

When she awoke, the bedroom was bright with sunlight, and someone was shaking her shoulder. "Good morning, sleepyhead," Mrs. O'Flaherty was saying.

Lulu rolled over. "Where's Miss Vi?" she asked. "I dreamed she went away last night, and Miss Alma came in."

"Not a dream," Mrs. O replied. "Vi is having breakfast, and if you hurry and get your clothes on, you can join her. I'll let her tell you about her adventure."

Lulu jumped up, and with Mrs. O'Flaherty's help, she quickly washed, dressed, and did her hair. When they entered the meeting room, Lulu saw Vi at one of the tables. A strange, stoop-shouldered man was seated opposite her, and though he was sitting down, Lulu had the impression that he was extremely tall.

Seeing Lulu, Vi motioned the girl forward. Lulu could now see another man at the table. His face and body were round, like balloons, and his cheeks were rosy red. He smiled instinctively at the sight of a child.

A Three-Ring Emergency

"Mr. Hedgegrow and Mr. Melanzana, I'd like you to meet my friend Lulu Raymond," Vi said.

The round man stood, and Lulu realized that he was nearly a head shorter than Miss Vi. He bowed and said, "Glad to meet you, Miss Lulu," in a high, cheery voice with an accent that sounded vaguely familiar to Lulu.

The other man didn't stand, and he didn't smile. He only nodded at Lulu, and she thought he looked sad.

"Mrs. Appleton has your breakfast waiting," Vi told her. "Go eat now, and I will join you soon."

Mrs. O'Flaherty went to the kitchen with Lulu, and indeed Mary was ready with a plate of scrambled eggs and bacon. "Where's everybody else?" Lulu inquired, realizing that the kitchen was empty except for herself and the two ladies.

"At the shelter," Mrs. O said. She poured a glass of milk for Lulu and a cup of coffee for herself.

"Who are those men? And why is the tall man so sad?" Lulu asked. She began to eat, but she didn't take her inquisitive eyes away from Mrs. O'Flaherty.

"You know that we decided yesterday to go to the circus on Saturday," Mrs. O began. "Well, last night, the circus came to us. The two gentlemen you just met are performers. In the circus, Mr. Hedgegrow is known as 'Eric the Giant' and Mr. Melanzana is 'Alonzo the Clown.' Mr. Melanzana owns the circus, though that doesn't mean much now. He's Italian, but he speaks English very well, except when he's excited."

Lulu's blue eyes had grown as round as saucers. *Circus performers! I just met real circus performers!* Lulu would not have been more thrilled if she had been introduced to the Queen of England.

Violet's Defiant Daughter

Mrs. O'Flaherty continued, "The circus wagons arrived in India Bay late yesterday afternoon, but something happened. Vi is getting the story now. What I gather is that the man who was the ringmaster and several other ruffians overpowered Mr. Melanzana, stole all his money, and then took the circus wagons and most of the animals, and left town. The performers were left with nothing but an old cart, one old horse, and the clothes on their backs. They were camping at the fairgrounds, which is about three miles from here. Apparently some boys, who had gone there in hopes of seeing the circus tents go up, told Mr. Melanzana about Samaritan House. The circus folks made their way here and knocked at our door in the wee hours."

Lulu was so engrossed in this amazing tale that she completely forgot her breakfast, until Mary said, "You eat those eggs, Lulu, and drink your milk. I don't want Miss Moran thinking I didn't feed you."

Lulu dug into her food again, and Mrs. O went on: "We didn't know what to do, until Vi decided that they should stay at the shelter until we can sort out their situation. There's plenty of room, and the house is almost finished. In answer to your question about where everybody else is this morning, Enoch, Christine, Alma, and Zoe are at the shelter, helping our new friends get settled. Rudy has gone to the market for supplies. Dr. Bowman has gone to the police station to report the theft. And Emily is minding the clinic. I will be helping the club ladies with the day nursery today."

"How many are there?" Lulu asked. "How many circus people?"

"About ten, I think," Mrs. O'Flaherty said.

"I guess I know why the tall man looks so sad," Lulu said.

A Three-Ring Emergency

"Actually, I think he always looks that way," said Mrs. O'Flaherty, "though he's very concerned about what will become of his friends, especially someone named Melissa."

"Miss Vi will fix everything for them," Lulu said confidently. She drank the last of her milk and took her glass and empty plate to the sink. "Can I help those people?"

"I'm sure you can, but we'll have to wait for Vi to tell us what to do," Mrs. O'Flaherty responded. "Gracious, look at the time. The club ladies will be here at any moment, and then the little ones will be arriving."

Mary put her hand on Lulu's shoulder and said, "You can help me, Lulu. Since Polly ain't here, will you find Jam, so I can feed her? That cat's probably lazing in Miss Vi's office, or she might be down in the cellar."

Lulu went to get the cat, but her imagination was full of the circus.

❧

Dr. Bowman had returned with Sergeant Peevy, a policeman who was a good friend of the mission, and the sergeant was getting all the information he needed from Mr. Melanzana and Mr. Hedgegrow.

"I can't promise you that we'll find 'em," Sergeant Peevy said as he closed his notebook, "but with four circus wagons, they should be easy to spot."

"Poor Melissa," said Mr. Hedgegrow in a voice so deep that it seemed to echo back on itself.

"Melissa?" said the sergeant. "You didn't say there's a woman with 'em." He flipped open his black book, prepared to take more notes for his investigation.

"Melissa's our tiger," Mr. Melanzana explained, "and Eric is quite attached to her. You should tell the other *polizie* that she's very old and gentle as a pussycat."

"She hasn't got no teeth," the tall man said mournfully, "and she wouldn't hurt nobody."

"I will include that in our information," said Sergeant Peevy. "I'll telegraph the sheriffs in all the counties around here; then I'll go out to the fairgrounds. Might find somebody who saw which direction those criminals took."

Vi showed the sergeant out, and a few minutes later, Dr. Bowman left with the circus men to go to the shelter. Several of the ladies of the club arrived as the men were leaving, but if they were surprised by the doctor's companions—one very tall and thin man with a long, sad face, and one very short and round man who doffed his hat and smiled affably—the ladies didn't show it. By now they had grown used to the interesting, and sometimes rather odd, people who flowed in and out of Samaritan House each day. Mrs. O'Flaherty greeted the volunteers at the door, and before anyone could ask, she explained about the circus and the robbery.

"I'm just glad Penelope wasn't with us," said Mrs. Kidd, the leader of the group, with a little wink at Mrs. O'Flaherty.

"Is Miss Pepper coming today?" Mrs. O asked.

"I'm afraid so," Mrs. Kidd replied, "but she always arrives a little late. She likes to make a grand entrance."

Mrs. O'Flaherty chuckled. "A grand entrance will be rather wasted today, for everyone who might observe her arrival is down at the shelter."

As it happened, Mrs. O'Flaherty was wrong. One person at the mission did see Miss Pepper's fine carriage arrive. Lulu was curled up in one of the large chairs on the front porch, reading *Around the World in Eighty Days* while she waited for Vi to return. She heard the carriage roll into the driveway and looked up to see who was in it. When Miss Pepper alighted, Lulu was tempted to run away. Instead, she held her breath, hoping that the lady would not notice her. Miss Pepper, with her nose pointed upward, looked neither right nor left as she crossed the porch and entered the house. *Why does she always look like she just smelled a skunk?* Lulu thought to herself. She looked toward the driveway, and a pair of eyes caught hers. The driver who had accused her of putting the firecrackers in the watermelon was glaring through the porch rails.

"I figured it was you," he said with an unpleasant smirk. "I recognized that yeller hair of yours right off. You might think you got away with something, girlie, but you ain't. I'm gonna see to it that Miz Pepper knows all about you."

Lulu didn't know what to say, but she felt a sudden urge to punch his ugly face. Instead, she stuck out her tongue at him. The man had turned away and didn't see her gesture. He climbed up to the driver's seat, flicked his whip at the horse, and drove away without turning his head.

Lulu was very angry, and also rather frightened. *What does he mean to do? Everybody knows I didn't pull the watermelon prank, so why's he being so hateful? Should I tell Miss Vi what he said?* This last question worried Lulu more than the others. She wanted to tell, because she was certain that Miss Vi would be angry too. But she didn't want to be a tattler. Besides, Miss Vi had enough problems at the moment. Lulu finally decided to keep the driver's words to herself. If she had talked it over with her wise Heavenly Friend, she might have made another choice. The driver's threat had made her feel as if she had done something wrong, though she knew she hadn't. She was so used to taking blame upon herself that she still could not comprehend that God could be so loving and forgiving that He would love and forgive her no matter what.

So Lulu did what she'd always done; she pushed the incident to the back of her mind, where it wouldn't trouble her.

⌒

"Does this mean there won't be a circus?" Lulu asked. She and Vi were in the mission buggy, which was over-flowing with items they were taking to the circus people.

"Not for a while," Vi replied. "But if the police catch the thieves, maybe Mr. Melanzana will recover his wagons, livestock, and equipment and start the circus again."

They reached the shelter, and Enoch and Zoe came to help carry the baskets and boxes inside. They all trooped into the house, where the first person to greet them was a handsome, dark-eyed woman dressed in gypsy attire. Her head was covered with a purple scarf that trailed down in the back. Her clothing consisted of layers of colorful items—a yellow blouse, a purple skirt over scarlet petticoats, a black vest embroidered in gold threads. Large gold hoops dangled from her ears, and metal bracelets jingled on her arms. Lulu had never seen such exotic attire, and she was instantly taken by Mrs. Melanzana.

Others came to help—a large, bald, muscular man called "Hercules," two pretty sisters who told Lulu that they were horseback riders, an older couple and their son who said they were tumblers and jugglers, and a very stout, very short lady who laughed heartily when she introduced herself as "Wanda the Wonder Woman." Lulu saw that several of them were dressed in costumes.

"We brought more clothing," Vi said, setting a large box on a table in the small sitting room that had once been Miss Moran's dining room.

"And lunch!" Zoe announced.

The circus folk helped carry the food baskets to the kitchen, but Vi asked the sisters — Mina and Ginna — to stay a moment. Vi took a thick bundle, wrapped in brown paper, and handed it to the girls. "I think these will fit," she said.

Mina and Ginna opened the package and carefully unfolded the clothing inside — skirts and blouses, two calico dresses, and undergarments of the softest cotton. There was also a paper bag containing brushes and combs, hair pins and ribbons, toothbrushes, and some lavender soap. The girls looked at Vi with tear-filled eyes. "You are so kind to us," Mina said in choked tones. "So kind," Ginna said, "and we can never repay you."

"You're our guests, and we want you to be comfortable," Vi replied simply.

Lulu had been watching this scene closely. She recognized the two calico dresses immediately; they were Miss Vi's very own! She was sure the rest of the things were from Vi's wardrobe as well. *Miss Vi gave her own clothes to the sisters!* Somehow, Lulu understood that Vi had done something very special. Vi barely knew the sisters, yet she had done what good friends do for one another. Lulu thought, *Miss Vi really is a Good Samaritan. I wish I could be like that. I'm glad I didn't tell her about that mean driver man and what he said. I don't want to make her unhappy.*

Then her nagging doubts said, *It's not such a big thing. Miss Vi has plenty of clothes. She won't miss a few old dresses.*

This time, Lulu got mad. "Oh, shut up and go away!" she exclaimed.

Fortunately, Vi and the young women had just gone to the kitchen and were out of earshot.

Accusations

*For by your words you will be
acquitted, and by your
words you will be
condemned.*

MATTHEW 12:37

Accusations

I guess this is turning out to be the best summer we ever had," Max was saying. He and Lulu were walking home from Willy Sturgis's house. Max, Lulu, Willy, Willy's sister, and a couple of the neighborhood boys had been playing an energetic game of tag after supper. Willy's father had finally sent everyone home when it became too dark to see.

"Yeah, the best," Lulu agreed, "except that Papa isn't here."

"But it's only three more weeks till he gets back, and there'll be lots of summer left," Max noted.

"When are you going back to Ion?" Lulu asked.

"Day after tomorrow," Max said. He picked up a stout stick that had fallen on the sidewalk and ran it along the posts of the fence in front of their house, making a funny clacking noise. "Mr. Ed is coming to town to get Miss Zoe, and he's going to pick me up. Do you want to go?"

Lulu thought a moment, then said, "Sometime, but I'm going back to the mission day after tomorrow. Polly's coming here, so Miss Vi invited me to stay overnight again. I'll get to visit with the circus people. They're really nice, and they tell such good stories 'bout the places they've been."

"How long are they going to stay at the shelter?"

"Miss Vi says as long as they need. They're still hoping to get their stuff back and start up the circus again."

"You really like going to the mission, don't you?" Max asked as they turned into their drive. "And you like Miss Vi now too, don't you?"

"I guess she's the nicest person I ever met," Lulu replied. "I like all the people at the mission."

"Say, have you seen that snobby lady again—the watermelon lady?" Max asked.

"Miss Pepper," Lulu said. "She comes to help with the day nursery, but I don't go around her. She's making Mrs. Appleton crazy with all her ideas about cooking and cleaning. Miss Vi says that Miss Pepper is even trying to get Dr. Bowman to change the way he runs the clinic."

"What does Miss Pepper know about clinics?" Max asked.

"Nothing, but Mrs. Appleton says Miss Pepper thinks she knows everything 'bout everything when really she doesn't know nothing 'bout nothing," Lulu answered with a giggle. "I just stay out of her way 'cause I don't want her telling me what to do."

"I don't blame you," Max said. "It's no use looking for trouble."

The next day, both children helped Kaki with chores at home, while Gracie accompanied Miss Moran on her weekly shopping. Max felt he should do whatever was needed around the house, since he was going to be away at Ion for a while. And Lulu—she had gotten into the habit of helping. The time she was spending with Vi at the mission was having an effect on her. Every day she saw the difficulties that some people faced in life and how her friends at the mission helped to ease the burdens through kindness and generosity. When the children had lived with their Aunt Gert, Lulu had resented the chores she was made to do. But Lulu had found a new role model. What Vi did at the mission, Lulu now wanted to do at home, by being helpful.

Accusations

Kaki and Miss Moran always expressed their appreciation for the children's work. For many of her ten years, Lulu had known little of praise and gratitude from her elders. Now others were planting new seeds and watering the seeds with their love and caring. In spite of Lulu's doubts, suspicions, and insecurities, God was making the seeds grow and take root in her heart.

It was three days later, and Lulu was sitting on the floor of Vi's office, playing with Jam. Her second overnight stay at the mission was going every bit as well as the first, though this time Lulu had slept peacefully. No unexpected guests had come to the door in the middle of the night.

The day before, when Ed Travilla had come to town to get Zoe and Max, he had brought some business papers for Vi, and now Vi was writing an important letter. One of the lessons Lulu had learned from her Papa was that sometimes just being quiet and letting another person concentrate was the best way to help. So Lulu was quietly tossing a yarn ball to the orange cat and waiting for Vi to finish her work.

After some minutes, Vi looked up from her writing and asked, "Lulu, would you go and find Mrs. O'Flaherty for me? I think she's in the nursery. If she's not too busy, I need her to help me with the wording of this letter."

Lulu got up quickly and said, "I'll find her, Miss Vi."

"Thank you," Vi said. Smiling so that her dimple appeared, she added, "I wonder how I got along without you, Lulu. You are such a help, and good company as well."

Lulu blushed at the compliment and left the office to find Mrs. O'Flaherty. Lulu ran across the kitchen, through a doorway, and into a narrow corridor. The mission residents often used this small, windowless hall as a shortcut. At one end was a high linen cupboard built in beneath the back stairs. At the other end, the corridor opened beneath the main stairway in the entrance hallway. The way the corridor was positioned under the front stairs created a blind spot, and after several accidental collisions, the residents of Samaritan House had learned to be very cautious when they exited the corridor. Lulu was aware of this, but in her hurry to fetch Mrs. O, she forgot to be watchful and rushed into the entry hall—running straight into Miss Penny Pepper.

Before Lulu could apologize, the startled Miss Pepper grabbed her arm and hissed, "Wretched child! Wretched little urchin!"

Lulu tried to pull herself free, but Miss Pepper's grip tightened. "You cannot escape me, you thoughtless brat—"

Miss Pepper stopped and stared into Lulu's upturned face. "Why, it's *you*," the tall woman said in surprise. "The girl with the yellow hair who was responsible for that disgraceful prank on the Fourth of July."

Miss Pepper bent forward so she was almost nose-to-nose with Lulu, and in a low, nasty tone, she said, "My footman described you in great detail. He told me all about what you did—how you made those little boys put the explosives in the watermelon and nearly kill me. You'll pay for that. I'll make you sorry."

"That's—that's not true! I—I—I didn't—" Lulu stammered.

"Don't deny it! Ralph would not lie to me. *You* are the liar! Little girls like you should be put in the workhouse where you can't harm good people anymore!"

Accusations

Lulu was struggling to get away, and she pulled at the woman's fingers.

"Ow! You've scratched me, you miserable child!" Miss Pepper yelped, but she didn't loosen her hold.

Seeing the bright red color of the woman's face, her puffed-out cheeks, and the fiery look in her small greenish eyes, Lulu suddenly thought that Miss Pepper might be a witch, and her struggle became desperate. Lulu's heart was pounding furiously, and the rush of blood in her ears drowned out all other sounds. With her free hand, she pushed with all her strength against Miss Pepper's vice-like hold on her arm. But the woman's strength was like iron.

In sheer panic, Lulu kicked out, and her booted foot landed a hard blow on Miss Pepper's shin. Lulu kicked again, harder this time, and at last, Miss Pepper released her.

Lulu was thrown backwards, landing hard on her tail-bone. The pain was so sudden and sharp that for an instant, she saw bright flashes of light, like stars. She wanted to get up, but she felt too light-headed. Somebody was yelling, "Stay where you are, Lulu! Don't move!"

It was Dr. Bowman. He had seen the end of the altercation and was tearing down the stairway to Lulu. He dropped to his knees beside her. With one arm firmly around her shoulders, he examined her spine with his other hand. He pressed different places and asked Lulu if she felt any pain. Then he held her neck and had her move her head from side to side. He told her to raise her arms and wriggle her fingers. Removing her boots, he instructed her to wriggle her toes. As scared as she was, Lulu thought the doctor's orders to wag her fingers and toes were funny. She was vaguely aware of other activity and heard a babble of ladies' voices, but she didn't pay attention to what they were saying.

Finally, Dr. Bowman said, "I don't believe any damage was done, Lulu. Let me help you." He raised her to her feet and again checked her spine. He told her to walk several steps, so he could observe her posture and her balance.

He smiled and said, "Your backside will be sore for a few days, and you might want to sit on a pillow. But you are not injured, my girl. I'm amazed that such a fall didn't bring tears, for I know it's painful."

"I guess I just forgot to cry," Lulu replied. In a whisper, she said, "I thought she might kill me, Dr. Bowman. I think she's a witch—a real one!"

Under his breath, the physician said, "Close enough to one."

Another arm came around Lulu's shoulders, and Vi said, "Come with me, darling. I want you to lie down, and Mary's bed is closest."

"I'll bring you some medicine that will make the pain better," Dr. Bowman promised, "right after I see to Miss Pepper."

Vi got Lulu onto Mary's bed.

"I ran into her by accident," Lulu said, "but I didn't do anything else, Miss Vi. She said I was a liar, and she'd send me to the workhouse."

Vi smoothed the hair back from Lulu's forehead and said, "I want to hear it all," she said, "but I must see Miss Pepper first. Enoch is bringing the carriage around so she can go home. You rest until I come back. I won't be long."

Lulu said, "I'm sorry 'bout the trouble."

"I'm sorry about your tailbone," Vi said. "Just let me get Miss Pepper on her way, and then you can tell me everything."

Accusations

Vi was gone for what seemed like a long time, and when she returned to Lulu's room she wasn't smiling. It wasn't anger that clouded her face, but worry.

Lulu, after taking Dr. Bowman's medicine and some tea, felt much better. Hearing the door open, she sat up and lowered her legs over the side of the bed.

"Don't get up quite yet," Vi said. "We need to have our talk. I want you to tell me exactly what happened with Miss Pepper."

Vi brought a small chair and set it next to the bed. She wanted to see Lulu's face as they talked. "You told me that you accidentally ran into Miss Pepper," Vi prompted.

"Yes, ma'am. I forgot to look when I ran out of that hall under the stairs," Lulu said. "I guess she was coming out of the nursery room. I ran out and bumped into her. It wasn't a hard bump, Miss Vi. I was going to apologize, but she grabbed my arm and wouldn't let go. She said I was a wretched something and other bad stuff."

"She grabbed you?" Vi asked in surprise. Penelope Pepper, who had told Vi her version of the incident in great detail, had not mentioned this.

"Yes, Miss Vi. See?" Lulu pushed back the sleeve of her dress and held out her left arm. The evidence was plain — a large red mark. Vi took Lulu's arm and gently turned it. She could clearly see finger marks on Lulu's skin.

"Does it hurt?" Vi asked.

"Naw," Lulu said. "Not now."

"What else did Miss Pepper say to you?"

"All kinds of mean things. She said that her driver man told her I was the one who made those boys put the firecrackers in the watermelon. She said I tried to kill her, and she's gonna send me to the workhouse. I tried to tell her the truth, Miss Vi, but she was yelling and holding me so tight that I couldn't get the words out. I thought she was a witch. I was scared, and I just wanted to get away from her!"

As Lulu spoke, she became quite agitated, and Vi moved from the chair to the bed. She took Lulu under her arm, and Lulu's tears finally fell. Vi held the trembling child and let her cry. When this wave of delayed emotion began to subside, Lulu said, "I'm sorry. I guess I got scared again, remembering what she said and her awful face."

Vi hugged Lulu and said, "You don't have to be sorry, darling. God gives us tears to help us wash away our fears and sorrows."

"I wish God would wash away Miss Pepper's meanness," Lulu replied fiercely.

"Tell me now, how did you get away from her grasp?" Vi asked.

"She was yelling, and I was pushing at her hand and trying to pull away. Then I fell backward. She didn't hit me or anything, she just let go."

"Did you kick her? Miss Pepper says that you kicked her, twice," Vi said in a plain way.

"I did kick her!" Lulu exclaimed. "That's why she let go of me! And then I fell down! I kicked her, and I'd do it again if she grabbed me like that!"

Vi sighed and said, "I believe I have the whole story now. Miss Pepper overreacted to a little accident, and she said cruel things to you. She had no right to grab you, and I shall tell her how wrong she was."

Accusations

Lulu smiled to herself. *I told the truth, and Miss Vi believes me! She'll tell that old witch off for good! That Miss Pepper's gonna be in big trouble—not me—and Miss Vi is on my side.*

Lulu wasn't entirely out of trouble, however. Vi returned to her seat on the little chair, and Lulu could see a strange look in her role model's eyes.

"Lulu, I am feeling very angry with Miss Pepper. But I am also disappointed in you," Vi said in a calm voice. "I know that you were frightened, but that is not an excuse for deliberately hurting Miss Pepper or anyone else. You probably didn't realize how hard you kicked, but the blows were strong enough to rip her stocking, cut her skin, and raise a knot on her leg. So you must take responsibility for her pain, regardless of how much she provoked you."

Some of the fear had returned to Lulu's eyes, but Vi saw another feeling there as well.

"I wanted to hurt her like she was hurting me!" Lulu declared defiantly.

Vi responded, "Jesus knows that it is not easy to refrain from striking out when someone threatens or hurts us. But He tells us that His way is to return evil and hatred with love. In Matthew 5: 39, He tells us, 'If someone strikes you on the right cheek, turn to him the other also.'

"Lulu," Vi continued, "if you hurt someone because that person hurt you—as Miss Pepper did—then you bring yourself down to her level. I know you can understand that. What Jesus is telling us is to answer hurt with love. It isn't easy. That's why it's so important that we let God into our hearts. He strengthens us in our weak moments. He helps us control our impulses to harm others or to wish harm on them. And He sends other people to help us when we are tempted to use violence."

Violet's Defiant Daughter

"Who was gonna help me?" Lulu demanded angrily.

Vi sat back in her chair and said, "Dr. Bowman was there when you fell. If you hadn't kicked Miss Pepper, he would have stopped her outburst and protected you."

"But I didn't know Dr. Bowman was there," Lulu protested, although the anger was fading from her voice.

"It's not for us to know God's plans, Lulu. It is for us to trust Him in everything," Vi replied. "If you will ask Him to forgive you for kicking Miss Pepper, He will forgive you. And if you trust in His love with all your heart, He will strengthen you to resist the temptation to hurt others. Talk to Him, dearest Lulu. You will never have a better friend than the Lord."

Lulu had lowered her head so that her chin rested on her chest. "Can you forgive me?" she asked.

"I have nothing to forgive you for," Vi said as she took the girl's hand.

Lulu looked up shyly and said, "I guess if I hadn't kicked her and if I'd waited for someone to help me, then my tailbone wouldn't be so sore."

Vi smiled and said, "You don't have to guess about that, Lulu. You were treated very unfairly today, but I think you've also learned something. When we hurt others, we hurt ourselves. The one thing you can do for me is to share your questions and your feelings with the Lord. Here now, let me help you up. The others have eaten lunch, but Mary has plates saved for us."

Lulu stood, and her back didn't feel so bad. Vi took a plump pillow from the bed and said, "I don't think Mary will mind if we take this for you to sit on."

As they went to the kitchen, Lulu asked, "Do you believe in evil witches, Miss Vi?"

"No, I don't," Vi said.

"I've decided that I don't either," Lulu said firmly. "I thought Miss Pepper was a witch. But she's not. I think she's a lady who doesn't know how to treat people. I think *she* needs to talk to Jesus about loving her neighbors."

Lulu didn't see Vi's smile.

That afternoon, Vi decided to take Lulu back to College Street earlier than planned. She needed to explain to Miss Moran what had occurred and to impart some instructions from Dr. Bowman, who wanted Lulu to avoid running and jumping for a couple of days.

Vi also had another call to make. She had determined to see Penny Pepper that very day. She didn't tell Lulu of her intentions. This was, Vi thought, a matter between herself and Miss Pepper. In truth, Vi was very angry—not at Lulu, but at a grown woman whose behavior to a child had been inexcusable. *How can we teach the children to have respect for adults when they see such an example?* Vi thought. *Penny has been spoiled all her life, and that's a shame. But I have to think of the children first. Penny has been generous to the day nursery with her time and her money, but not with her heart. I can't let this situation continue.*

Vi was not the kind of person who invited confrontations, so she wasn't looking forward to seeing Penelope Pepper. As she drove her buggy toward the Pepper estate, she prayed for guidance: *Lord, help me say the right things. Help me listen with love and speak with understanding. Help me not to fall into accusations and rebukes. And please, give me the strength to check my temper. However this conversation goes, let me remember to abide by everything I told Lulu today.*

Violet's Defiant Daughter

Arriving at the mansion, Vi was admitted by an elderly butler. He informed her that Mr. and Mrs. Pepper were not at home, but Vi said that she had come to see Miss Pepper. At this, the butler raised his eyebrows in a questioning way—as if Penny Pepper didn't often have visitors. Quickly recovering his bland composure, he showed Vi into a sumptuous parlor, where Miss Pepper was reclining on a brocade-covered couch. She was attired in a costly silk dressing gown. Her leg was propped on a pillow, a bag of ice on her "wound," and she was pressing a cologne-soaked handkerchief to her temple. A maid hovered close by, awaiting her mistress's next command. Far from the red-faced woman who had left the mission in a rage just hours before, Miss Pepper now languished like the sentimental heroine of a silly romance novel—too weak, she said, to rise.

Vi had to employ all her speaking skills (and several silent prayers for patience) to convince Miss Pepper that Ralph, the footman, had been "mistaken" in his version of the Fourth of July prank and that Lulu Raymond was not involved—indeed, that Lulu had also been a victim of the boys' mischief. Miss Pepper would have none of it until Vi mentioned that Lulu was not a child of Wildwood but the daughter of Professor Marcus Raymond, the new head of classical studies at India Bay University.

This new information appealed to Penny Pepper's pretentious snobbery, and she finally allowed that she had, perhaps, been "a bit hard on the child." Miss Pepper even said that she might owe the child an apology for her misjudgment, and she suggested that she could pay a call to the Raymond home, when the professor was present, and speak to him and young Lulu. She was visibly disappointed when she learned that Professor Raymond was out of the country and would not return for several weeks.

"Then perhaps I will write the dear little girl a note, just to let her know that I forgive her behavior today," Miss Pepper condescended.

"That would be appropriate," Vi said, almost choking on her words but keeping her tone even.

Before leaving, Vi thanked Miss Pepper for her generosity to the day nursery. "But I am afraid your talents are being wasted in caring for small children," Vi said. "There is something else that might be more fitting for your skills and your interests. I've read lately about the cooking schools that have been started in New York and Boston."

"Oh, yes, I know all about them," Miss Pepper replied with interest. "A most worthwhile enterprise — training for hired cooks in the culinary science and classes for poor and working women in healthful and hygienic cookery."

"Would not so worthy an enterprise benefit the people of India Bay?" Vi asked.

"I've thought of that myself, Violet, many times," Miss Pepper said, though in truth she had never before had such a thought.

Vi continued, "With your knowledge of household science and your organizational skills, there could be no one better to plan such a school for India Bay. Of course, it would be a major undertaking, and I know that you have many other duties. . ."

"I would have to give up my volunteer days at your mission," Miss Pepper mused, "although it is not very demanding work, you know, looking after those poor children."

Vi bit down on her tongue to stop herself from responding. *What Miss Pepper knows about caring for children can be put in a thimble with room to spare!*

"I will do it, Violet, for the benefit of our fellow citizens," Miss Pepper declared.

"I'm so glad," Vi said, and no statement had ever been more true.

"You will wish to be kept abreast of my progress?" Miss Pepper asked, but before Vi could reply, Miss Pepper began issuing orders to her maid: "Hattie, get my address book. And my writing desk. Go, go!"

Hattie hurried out, aiming a sly smile at Vi on her way.

"Thank you for coming, Violet," Miss Pepper said, dismissing her guest.

Vi had turned to the door when Miss Pepper added, "Do let me know when Professor Raymond returns to the city. My father is on the board of the university, and I know he would like to meet the professor. I hear he is rather young and a widower."

"I will keep in touch," Vi said, and she left.

In her little buggy once more, driving southward toward Wildwood, Vi finally let herself relax. She hadn't realized how tense she was. *What in the world made me think of a cooking school?* she asked herself. She had read several magazine articles about the Eastern schools but had not thought much about them. The idea had just popped into her head, and it was a good idea. She chuckled about how the situation had been resolved.

In this mood of happiness, she thought, *Dear Lord, what miracles You have wrought today! Penelope Pepper admitted she was in the wrong. I held my temper. She will no longer be underfoot at the mission! And we might even get a cooking school in India Bay. Most important to me is that Lulu was not badly hurt. Lord, please continue to keep Your watch over her. I know that her heart is opening to the fullness of Your love, but it is so difficult for her to trust. Some fear holds her back. You know her true heart. Guide her, Lord, upon Your joyful path. And forgive me for my feelings of anger toward Miss Pepper.*

Vi did feel that she was on a joyful path. Today, she had expressed her disappointment to Lulu. She had talked to Lulu as a mother would. Perhaps, Vi thought, they had achieved a breakthrough, and her hope to earn Lulu's trust was being fulfilled.

CHAPTER

An Early Warning

*Watch out that you do not
lose what you have
worked for. . .*

2 JOHN 8

An Early Warning

ollowing Dr. Bowman's instructions, Miss Moran gave Lulu a dose of medicine just before bed. The concerned housekeeper checked the child a couple of hours later and was relieved to find Lulu sleeping peacefully. Reassured, Miss Moran went to her own rest. She had decided to sleep in Max's vacant room, in case Lulu needed her during the night.

Sometime later, Lulu half-woke with a feeling that something was wrong. Her back ached, and she turned this way and that. In her discomfort, she wondered if she should call Miss Moran. But the doctor had said she would be sore for a while, and Lulu didn't feel sick or feverish. She prided herself on her toughness, often to a fault, so she decided to be strong. After much shifting, she found a position in which her back felt better, and she closed her eyes in hopes of getting to sleep again.

Awake now, her mind did not want to sleep. It brought up memories of what had caused her pain and revived her angry emotions. Behind her closed eyelids, she could see again Miss Pepper's red face and hear her hateful accusations. For the first time since the incident, Lulu clearly recalled how forcefully she had kicked and the stunned look on Miss Pepper's face. Then the ugly Miss Pepper seemed to fade into Miss Vi, and Lulu saw the expression of disappointment on her role model's face. That had felt worse than anything Miss Pepper did or said.

An angry thought crossed Lulu's mind. *Why was Miss Vi disappointed in me? Didn't she understand that I had no choice? The witch was going to hurt me. What else could I have done? It wasn't fair for Miss Vi to lecture me like that. Not fair at all.*

The better part of Lulu wanted to argue against the thoughts, but the doubts took advantage of Lulu's fatigue and pain to whisper more. *If Miss Vi really loved me, she'd never have said those things. She's not my mother. What right did she have to lecture me with all that "turn the other cheek" stuff? She didn't see what happened. She didn't know how mean that Miss Pepper was being. Would a real friend have lectured me like that, when I didn't deserve it? Maybe Miss Vi is just a fair-weather friend. Maybe under her niceness, she's just like Aunt Gert, and I shouldn't trust her so much.*

Lulu tried to push the thoughts away, but doubt preys on the weak, and Lulu was weak in a way she didn't understand. Her own will wasn't strong enough to combat her doubts. But the gentle arm of sleep at last stilled her thoughts and calmed her troubled soul with a dream of her father. In her dream, her Papa was home again, and she was happy.

When she awoke the next morning, she did indeed feel sore. But Miss Moran brought her breakfast in bed, and Gracie came in to sit with her. They decided to spend the day together, like they used to do. They would read to each other, and later on, they would play with Gracie's paper dolls.

Lulu didn't remember much about waking in the night, but she had the strange sensation that something had bothered her. Something about Miss Vi and a fair-weather friend? Whatever it was, Lulu was glad to stay home with Gracie that day. She didn't really want to go back to the mission until she felt better.

An Early Warning

Vi didn't expect to see Lulu or Gracie for a day or two. She knew that Dr. Bowman wanted Lulu to rest, and the little girl could do that better at home, where Miss Moran and Kaki could keep her still. Vi had many tasks to attend to, but her thoughts were always with the Raymond children and their father. Mark would be returning soon, and Vi was feeling confident that he would find a happy family waiting for him. She could now envision herself as part of that family, and she began to indulge her imagination with visions of a wedding at Ion. Her Grandpapa would give her away, Zoe and Rosemary would be her bridesmaids, and Ed would stand with Mark.

"What has brought out that dimple of yours?" Mrs. O'Flaherty asked. She had come upon Vi sorting some donated clothing.

Vi looked up at her dear friend and said, "I was thinking about the future."

"Do your thoughts include a wedding?" Mrs. O teased.

"That very thing," Vi replied. "I shouldn't let myself become so imaginative when we do not even know the date of the event. But I am so sure now that nothing will stand in our way."

"Not even a certain little girl?" Mrs. O'Flaherty asked.

"I really think that Lulu and I are making great progress," Vi said. "She's an amazing girl, and I believe she will grow into an extraordinary woman. All of them amaze me — Max, Gracie, and Lulu. I feel privileged to be a part of their lives."

"Lulu does seem to be a magnet for trouble, and only some of it of her own making," Mrs. O'Flaherty noted with a small chuckle. "She is a complicated child, and I think she will always be spirited, which is a blessing when it is restrained by good judgment and common sense. I have seen how Lulu relates to you now, Vi, and she has certainly come a long way since that day of the frogs. I believe that you have become her role model, as well as her friend."

Vi blushed and replied, "I hope I may influence her to find a higher model. Above everything else, Mrs. O, I want her to know Jesus as her Lord and Savior. I want her to experience the great adventure of faith, and I believe she is truly opening herself to His love and His gift of grace."

Mrs. O said, "Stay strong for her, and don't become disheartened if she slips backwards at times. Young Lulu has relied on herself for so long that it cannot be easy for her to surrender her will to our Lord."

"Do you anticipate more problems?" Vi asked in concern.

"I try not to anticipate anything," Mrs. O'Flaherty said with a gentle smile. "I just want you to be prepared. A child like Lulu, so strong-willed and imaginative, may be prone to slipping back into old ways, so you should be alert. To be prepared for problems is not the same as assuming there will be problems. That's all I'm saying."

"That's what a parent does, isn't it, to protect her child," Vi said thoughtfully.

"Parents cannot protect children against all their mistakes. Nor should they, for we must make mistakes in order to learn and improve. But a loving parent is watchful. Now, let me help you with this sorting. It reminds me of our first visit to Lansdale. Do you remember when we cleaned out your Aunt Wealthy's little guesthouse?"

An Early Warning

Mrs. O'Flaherty's recollection sparked a mirthful conversation about their visit to Ohio five years earlier. But Vi did not forget Mrs. O's words of warning.

Max returned from Ion tanned and exhilarated. When he learned what had happened to Lulu, he was very solicitous and went out of his way to find things for her to do while she was "laid up," as Kaki said. He taught her some new games and took his turn reading to both his sisters. He told them stories about Ion, including how he had ridden Galahad, Mr. Ed's vigorous horse, in the paddock.

By the fourth day after her fall, Lulu's soreness had almost gone, and Max suggested that they visit the mission again. He wanted to meet the circus folks, and Gracie was anxious to see Polly. Lulu agreed, though she felt a little shy about seeing Miss Vi. She couldn't explain this feeling to herself, so she quickly dismissed it.

Elwood drove the children to Samaritan House that afternoon, and Vi was overjoyed to see them. Gracie had brought her paper dolls, and she and Polly were soon at play in Polly's room. Vi invited Lulu and Max to go with her to the shelter, and they didn't need to be asked twice. As they walked down Wildwood Street, Vi informed the children that the circus wagons and horses had been found by a farmer in a county at the far west of the state.

"What about Melissa?" Lulu asked. "Is she okay?"

"Apparently the farmer is taking good care of her," Vi said. "He was afraid at first, but he gave her food and water. When he saw how gentle she was, he let her out of her cage and put her on a leash."

Violet's Defiant Daughter

Confused, Max asked, "Who's Melissa? Why was she in a cage? Is she some kind of wild woman?"

Lulu broke into laughter and said, "She's a tiger! Melissa is very special to Mr. Hedgegrow, the tall man. He must be very happy now."

"Oh, he is," Vi said. "I believe I even saw him smile when Sergeant Peevy told him the news. Mr. Hedgegrow, Mr. Melanzana, and Mr. Hercules are going today to retrieve the wagons and Melissa. I have train tickets for them." Vi patted her pocket.

"So the circus people will be leaving here soon?" Lulu asked with a sigh.

"Not for a while," Vi said. "They must get the wagons back here and see what equipment they will need. The sheriff in Weston County couldn't tell what had been stolen because he didn't know what was in the wagons. But his telegram said 'wagons, horses, tents, ropes, and tiger,' so we are hoping that the thieves just abandoned everything. If their losses are not too great, Mr. Melanzana hopes to stage performances in India Bay before the circus moves on."

They'd reached the shelter, and Mrs. Melanzana opened the door when Vi knocked. Seeing Lulu, the woman hugged her and said, "Are you better, my child? Miss Travilla told us what happened to you. We were all so worried about you."

Lulu grinned and said, "I'm fine, thank you." She introduced Max, and to his disconcerted surprise, Mrs. Melanzana grabbed him in a hug too.

"Welcome, Max," she said gaily. "Any brother of Lulu's is a friend of ours. Now come out to the kitchen with me, while Miss Travilla talks to my husband. He's in the sitting room, Miss Vi, with Eric and Hercules."

An Early Warning

Vi went to find the circus owner, and Lulu and Max followed Mrs. Melanzana. In the new kitchen building, two pretty girls were making lemonade, and a large woman sat in a rocking chair, fanning herself. Mrs. Melanzana introduced Max to the girls, Mina and Ginna, and the woman, whom she identified as Miss Smiley.

"Just call me 'Wanda,'" the large woman laughed. "I haven't been Miss Smiley since I ran away with the circus."

When the lemonade was ready, Mina and Ginna asked Max to help them take glasses to the Garibaldi family.

"They're acrobats," Mina said. "And jugglers," Ginna added.

Mrs. Melanzana poured lemonade for Lulu, Wanda, and herself, and the women told Lulu more of their circus tales—such as the night their monkeys got loose in a boardinghouse in St. Louis (the circus gave all but the laziest of the monkeys to a zoo after that), and the time Wanda became stuck in a revolving door in a hotel in Richmond and some firemen had to take the door apart to rescue her. When Mrs. Melanzana made a remark about telling fortunes, Lulu, remembering the woman's exotic costume on the first day they met, asked, "Are you really a gypsy? Can you see into the future?"

Mrs. Melanzana's dark eyes sparkled as she said, "No and no. I'm really a farm girl from New Hampshire. I met Mr. Melanzana when he came to the farm to buy vegetables, and he made me laugh when he told me that he was an eggplant. That's what 'melanzana' means in Italian. So I'm a farm girl who became Mrs. Eggplant. I did tell fortunes for a while. Now I sell tickets and cook, but I still wear the costume because I love dressing in bright colors."

"But why did you stop telling fortunes?" Lulu asked.

"I started reading the Bible, and I realized that it is wrong for me to pretend to know something I don't," Mrs. Melanzana replied simply.

"Do you have a house somewhere?" Lulu asked.

Wanda laughed. "We're traveling people, Lulu. The circus is our home, and we're one big family. You must have noticed that we're all a little *different* from everyday folks" — she winked at Lulu — "and all of us have a lot of wanderlust."

"My family's different," Lulu said suddenly. "Our Mamma died, and my brother and sister and me had to live with our aunt for a long time. Now we have our Papa to care for us, and we're a family again."

Mrs. Melanzana looked thoughtfully at Lulu. "I am very sorry you lost your mother," the woman said gently. "It's a painful thing to lose a parent."

"Yes, ma'am, it is," Lulu said a little too matter-of-factly. "But I don't talk about it much."

"Sometimes it helps to talk about our sorrows," Mrs. Melanzana said. She was going to say something else, but she saw that Lulu was fidgeting uncomfortably. She understood instinctively that the child had not meant to speak of her mother, and the subject was obviously the source of heartache. So Mrs. Melanzana quickly changed the topic. "If you're finished with your drink, Lulu, I'll take you out to see the Garibaldis practice."

Lulu jumped up and took Mrs. Melanzana's hand. She was glad the conversation about families had ended.

Returning to the mission, Vi asked the children to sit with her in the meeting room for a few minutes. Vi said,

An Early Warning

"It's time to send your letters to your father. The postman has told me that if we mail the letters tomorrow, they will reach Mexico City before your Papa returns from the expedition—with several days to spare. Bring your letters when you come tomorrow. We'll put them in a large, strong envelope that I purchased at the stationery store and take them to the post office. Does that suit you?"

"Oh, goody!" Gracie exclaimed. "That means Papa will be home soon! When is he coming, Miss Vi?"

"According to his plan, your father is scheduled to arrive two weeks from today."

"We can mark the days off on the calendar Miss Moran keeps in the kitchen," Lulu suggested. "It'll be fun to watch the days go by."

Then Vi took a folded sheet of paper from her pocket and said, "This came from my brother Ed this morning. It's an invitation to a birthday party for my Mamma. Ed wants you to go to Ion with Mrs. O'Flaherty and me and to stay for the whole weekend of the party. Would you like that?"

This elicited an excited chorus of yeses, and Max asked when the visit would take place. "The weekend before your father comes home," Vi said. "We will return from Ion on Sunday, and he will arrive the next day."

"I wish Papa could be here for the party," Gracie said a little sorrowfully.

"So do I," Vi said. "Ed says the same in his letter, but he was very firm about the date. I think he's planned a special surprise for Mamma. He's being very mysterious, but he writes that the party must be on August ninth, though Mamma's birthday is actually a day earlier." She held out the letter so the children could see it and pointed to a line.

Violet's Defiant Daughter

"Look, he has underlined the date three times and added an exclamation point."

"How old will your mother be?" Gracie asked.

Lulu nudged her little sister and said, "Nobody's supposed to ask a lady's age."

Smiling, Vi said, "That's true most of the time, Lulu. But my Mamma has never been bothered by telling her age. She'll be fifty years old."

Lulu let out a little whistle and said, "That sounds old, but your mother doesn't look old. Not at all. Are you sure that's her age?"

"As sure as I can be," Vi laughed. "What I don't know is what Ed has up his sleeve for her party. Miss Zoe will be there with my grandparents. Tansy and Marigold, of course, and lots of my aunts, uncles, and cousins are coming. There will be many young people for you to meet. So may I write to Ed and tell him that we will attend?"

"Yes, please," Max said, speaking for himself and his sisters.

"We can mark those days on the calendar, too," Lulu said with a grin. "I guess we've got lots of good things to look forward to."

CHAPTER

A Breaking Storm

*. . .and call upon me in the
day of trouble; I will deliver
you, and you will
honor me.*

PSALM 50:15

A Breaking Storm

*S*ummer in India Bay was steaming hot, but the Raymond children did not mind. In June, they'd come to anticipate afternoon storms—heralded by low, growling, distant thunder—that passed over the city in dark downpours, leaving rainbows in their wake and keeping gardens green and blooming. Miss Moran told them that July and August would be hotter and drier, and her forecast was correct. For weeks, there had been almost no rain, and the brief showers that visited the city did little more than stir up the dust in the streets. But life went on, and people made do, waiting for the storm season that usually began in August.

One morning in the first week of the month, the Raymond children arrived to find workmen erecting tall poles on the street outside the mission. Vi and Mrs. O'Flaherty were talking with a man who kept pointing up at the poles. Lulu and Gracie recognized Mr. Gibbons, whom they had met at the Lansings' tea party.

Elwood said he would return in the afternoon. He was going to the butcher shop to help his father, and he promised to bring back a big beef roast for Miss Moran—news that made Max's mouth water, for he was especially fond of Miss Moran's roast dinners.

Vi greeted the children, and naturally, they wanted to know about the wooden poles. "It's so exciting," Vi said. "Samaritan House is getting a telephone—the first telephone in Wildwood. Those men raising the poles are Mr. Gibbons's employees."

Mr. Gibbons was happy to see the girls again and to meet Max. When Max asked how the telephone would work, Mr. Gibbons began to explain about the installation and the wiring and how voices could travel along the wire from one place to another. With regret, Vi excused herself. She needed to see Dr. Bowman and Emily about an order of medical supplies. Then she would visit the shelter. Mr. Melanzana and the other men had returned with the circus wagons late the previous night, and Vi didn't yet know how much of their stolen goods had been recovered and what they would require to get the circus going again, although she had already decided to invest some of her personal funds in the Melanzana Circus. After that, she would meet with Mrs. Kidd about plans to recruit more volunteers for the day nursery. So she left the children in Mrs. O'Flaherty's capable hands for the rest of the morning.

Vi quickly finished her meeting in the clinic and hurried off to the shelter. As she walked down the block, she felt a hot wind blowing from the direction of the ocean. Looking upward, she saw no sign of clouds. She hoped the hot wind was the harbinger of rain, for the dryness of July had become the drought of August. Not a drop had fallen in two weeks, and Vi was very worried about the water situation in Wildwood.

She received mostly good news at the shelter. The circus wagons were in good condition, as were the horses. Melissa was no worse for wear, and Mr. Hedgegrow was pampering the toothless old tiger with bowls of milk and sweet corn mush. But the circus's exotic birds, including a talking parrot, two monkeys, and smaller animals, had been set loose by the thieves. Several of the sideshow exhibits had been destroyed, the store of canned foods and animal feed had been taken, and, of course, Mr. Melanzana's cashbox and all his savings had been stolen.

A Breaking Storm

Vi made her investment offer, and after some protests that she had done too much already, Mr. Melanzana accepted. "Since you are now a stockholder, you must let me pay you a dividend," the grateful circus owner said. "Tomorrow we will move to the fairgrounds again, if it does not rain too much. It will be easier to make the necessary repairs where we can unfold the tents. We may be ready in another week, and our little family has agreed that the Melanzana Circus will perform—one day only—just for the people of Wildwood. There will be no charge for anything. Do you think the people would enjoy this, Miss Travilla? Do you think they will attend?"

His offer had taken Vi's breath away. "Enjoy—attend?" she stammered. Tossing the rules of etiquette aside, she threw her arms about the round, jolly man. "It's such a wonderful thing! I am overwhelmed by your generosity! God bless you, Mr. Melanzana. God bless all of you!"

"It will be a somewhat smaller circus than the one we brought to India Bay, but I guarantee a fine show," Mr. Melanzana said. "You come back tomorrow morning, before we leave, and we will discuss the details, eh? But you should go back to the mission now. I feel a change in the air, and I think the big rain is coming."

Almost dancing out the shelter door, Vi waved to Mr. Melanzana and called out, "If it does storm, bring the horses to our stable."

Mr. Melanzana stepped outside, watching Vi as she went down the street. "God bless that young woman," he said fervently. "She is one of the saints."

He walked into the yard and looked up. The sky had turned a peculiar gray-green in the east, and the wind was stronger. Mr. Melanzana, who had grown up in a fishing village in his native Italy, frowned. "We'd better take the horses to the mission stable," he said to himself, "and move Melissa's cage into the washroom."

~~~~~

While Vi was away, Max had remained glued to Mr. Gibbons's side, and Mr. Gibbons greatly enjoyed the boy's company and his many questions. But seeing that the girls were losing interest, Mrs. O'Flaherty took them in to find Polly, and they went up to the schoolroom. After a while, Lulu asked if she might read. She had finished *Around the World in Eighty Days*, and Vi had lent her another of Mr. Verne's novels. Gracie and Polly were playing a noisy game of circus, inspired by their friends at the shelter, so Mrs. O'Flaherty suggested that Lulu go to Vi's office, where it was quiet.

Lulu took her book and went downstairs. In the entrance hall, she stopped and listened to the laughing voices of small children coming from the nursery. *It's a good thing I don't have to watch out for Miss Pepper anymore*, she thought. *Miss Vi said she won't be coming back here anytime soon.*

Instead of using the little corridor, Lulu walked through the meeting room, where several elderly women were sitting and talking. Lulu said "Hello" and made a quick curtsy.

"Good to see ya, girl," the Widow Amos said. "Where ya headed?"

Lulu held out her book and said, "To Miss Vi's office, ma'am, so I can read."

"Good on ya! Never learned readin' myself, but I wish I had. Now you stay inside. There's a storm brewing. I can feel it in these old bones."

The old lady slapped her knees, and Lulu giggled.

A Breaking Storm

"I'll stay in," Lulu said, and she went to the kitchen, where Mary was helping the church ladies prepare the day's food baskets. Lulu heard Mrs. Stephens say something about getting their deliveries finished before the storm broke. Not wanting to interrupt, Lulu went straight to Vi's office. She thought Jam might be there, but the cat had retreated to the cellar. The office seemed stuffy, and Lulu raised the window. Then she stretched on the rug, opened her book, and turned her active mind to the story of island castaways currently under attack by pirates. So engrossed was Lulu that she didn't notice how the light was changing in the room.

A loud swooshing sound broke her concentration, and she looked up to see the lacey window curtains blowing straight out from the wall. As she watched, the curtains suddenly dropped down. A few seconds passed, and the gusting wind blew the curtains up again and rattled the window panes. A shower of papers was blown off Miss Vi's desk and drifted to the floor. The wind quieted, and Lulu got to her knees, gathering the fallen papers into a neat bundle. She laid the papers on Vi's desk chair, with her book on top as a paperweight. The wind blew again, and a few more papers fell from the desk. Making a game of it, Lulu scrambled to catch them before they reached the floor.

She saw that they were pages of a letter, and she tried to put them in order. It was then she recognized the writing on the pages as her father's. *It must be a letter to me and Max and Gracie, but why is it here?* She riffled the sheets, looking for the first page. There it was—a page beginning "My dearest, darling..."

Lulu's heart seemed to jump into her throat. Her face was suddenly hot and damp.

Violet's Defiant Daughter

Again, she read the words her Papa had written: "My dearest, darling Vi."

Fighting panic, Lulu read more. Her racing pulse began to slow. The first page contained much the same information as had her Papa's letter to his children—where he was, who was with him, where they were going in Yucatan. "It's only a friendly letter," she said. "Maybe grown-ups call their friends 'dear' and 'darling.' That's okay, I guess."

But Lulu's doubts whispered, *Read on.*

She turned to the second page, and her heart began to hammer once more. Terrible words seemed to leap out at her—*engagement, marriage, wedding!* She didn't read everything. She decided she was mistaken; her father couldn't have written this. She looked at the last page. There was his signature and above it, words that struck Lulu harder than any physical blow:

How I long for the day when we are husband and wife, dear Vi. Until that day, hold my love in your heart and know that you have made me happier and more blessed than any man has a right to be.

Mark

Lulu angrily crumpled the pages in her fist and hurled them away from her. She was in a real state of panic now. The brewing storm outside was nothing in comparison to the chaos of her emotions. *It's all true!* she thought desperately. *Everything I was afraid of, it's true! Miss Vi has been deceiving us, pretending to be our friend so she can steal our Papa away. I hate her so much! What can I do? I can't stay here! I've got to get away! I don't ever want to see Miss Vi, not ever again!*

A Breaking Storm

Lulu leapt up and went to the window. The wind was cool against her hot skin, but it only made her feel dizzy. She looked out and saw someone coming in the back gate of the mission grounds. It was Miss Vi, returning from the shelter! Lulu jumped back from the window, so she couldn't be seen.

She'll be here any minute. I have to get away!

Lulu went to the window again and peeked out. She couldn't see Miss Vi, so she climbed onto the wide ledge and swung her feet over. In a flash, she thought of Jam, the gentle orange cat who usually occupied the window ledge, and of everything she was leaving behind. She sat still, unmoving and undecided. But the sound of women's voices came from the kitchen, and Lulu's panic returned. She scooted to the edge of the window and dropped down.

There was a mossy patch beneath the window that softened her fall. The window ledge was just above her head. The wind died down for a moment, and Lulu heard a door bang. A voice—Miss Vi's voice!—came clearly to Lulu's ears: "I thought I closed that window." Then the window was shut and locked.

Did she see me? Gotta run! Gotta get away!

Lulu dashed across the graveled drive toward the hedges that lined the boundary between the mission and the side street. She made her way to the back gate, and spotting no one around, she ran out. *Where now?* Lulu thought about the shelter, and a notion of running away with the circus struck her. But that wouldn't work. The circus people would just bring her back to the mission. She'd have to go eastward, down the side street and away from the mission.

She didn't know the street's name or where it went, but she had a vague idea that it might lead to the railway yards.

Violet's Defiant Daughter

In a confused way, she thought about getting on a train going north to Kingstown and finding Mrs. Greeley, her Papa's kind landlady who'd taken care of the children before the family moved to India Bay.

Lulu had gone a couple of blocks when she realized that the wind was getting stronger, and she was running against it. It whipped at her skirts and her hair, and it seemed to be pushing her back toward the mission. There was a great deal of dust and debris in the air. She stopped to get her bearings. No one was following her. A few people were outside their houses. She saw a man latching his house shutters. In another yard, a woman was chasing chickens, shooing them into a cellar door.

A dustman's cart suddenly came round a corner. The driver cracked his whip, and his horse broke into a run, churning up more gritty dirt. Lulu's eyes stung, but she saw something fall from the cart. She grabbed the thing—a square piece of oilcloth, tattered but sturdy, that had once covered a table in somebody's kitchen. *I'll keep it*, she thought, *to cover my head if it rains*.

Tired from fighting the wind, she turned southward into a narrow, twisting alleyway. A long wooden fence ran down one side of the alley and provided some refuge from the wind. Lulu slowed to a walk. Her run had dampened her anger somewhat, and she was thinking a little more clearly. *I have to find a place to go.*

The sun was now hidden by roiling gray clouds, and it was growing darker. The alley was deeply rutted and pocked with large rocks. It was harder to see, and she stumbled a couple of times. Then she fell over a rock, scraping her knees on the hard ground. But she ignored the stinging cuts and trudged on. Lulu didn't know that the long alley was taking her back to Wildwood Street until she reached the end and saw, on the opposite side of the street, the dry goods store and the greengrocer's, where she'd gone several times with Miss Vi and Mrs. O'Flaherty. Lulu almost cried when she remembered the day that Miss Vi had bought hair ribbons for her and Gracie and Polly from the dry goods lady. Miss Moran had tied her braid with one of the ribbons that very morning. Lulu reached behind and touched her hair, but the ribbon was gone. Lulu was always losing her ribbons, but for some reason, this loss nearly broke her heart.

Something wet hit her nose, and she looked upward. The rain was beginning, falling in big, heavy drops that made a plopping sound when they hit the baked, dusty ground. There were only a few drops at first, but Lulu knew they would become a deluge. She looked in every direction. Turning back to the alley, she saw what might be a barn. She'd walked by it without noticing. Draping the oilcloth over her head, for the rain was coming faster, she ran to the building. It was a barn, but the big doors were bolted with a wooden plank, and she couldn't lift it. It had gotten so dark she could barely see. The rain was now pelting her oilcloth, and she was very scared.

A huge bolt of lightning streaked across the black sky, startling Lulu but revealing a small door near the large ones. She made her way to where she thought the door was and felt around until her hand touched a metal latch. The metal was wet and her hand slipped, but she tried again, and it lifted. She pushed, and the door swung open.

The smells of horses, mixed with the sweet, dry aroma of hay and the sharp odor of manure, hit her nose, and she knew instantly that the building was a stable. She could hear horses neighing and pawing at the ground. The clatter of iron-clad hooves against wood made her jump in fear. Then she realized that the horses were reacting to the storm by pawing at their stall doors. She didn't know what time it was but guessed it might be about one o'clock in the afternoon. Yet it was nearly as dark as night inside the stable. Another streak of lightning lit the building for an instant, and Lulu saw that the light came from a small window not far from where she was standing. She dropped the oilcloth and stretched her arms out in front of her. Taking shuffling baby steps, she cautiously moved toward the window, until her foot struck something that felt hard but shifted strangely when she poked it again with her foot. She stood motionless and waited for the next lightning strike. When it came, she saw that she was standing in front of an untidy pile of large feed bags.

She collapsed onto the pile. The rough burlap was scratchy against her arms, but the smell of corn and clover emanating from the bags was pleasant and somehow soothing. "I can wait out the storm here," Lulu said aloud. "When it's light again, I'll decide where to go."

Thanks to the oilcloth, her hair and most of her clothing were dry, but her feet and calves were soaked. So Lulu unlaced her boots and kicked them off. She peeled off her wet stockings. The feed bags formed something like a large chair, and she shifted around until she was comfortable. She could see the lightning through the little window over her head. The rain was pounding the stable roof, and each bolt of lightning was now followed immediately by a thunderclap, drowning out the sounds of the frightened horses.

Exhausted by the emotional turmoil of reading her father's letter, her desperate escape into the storm, and her search for safety, Lulu couldn't think about anything. For once, her imagination refused to conjure up images that might distract her. She could only watch the window for bursts of white light and listen to the raging storm.

~~~~~~~

It was about the time that Lulu was making her way down the alley that Vi discovered her missing. Nobody knew where she was. Vi's hurried search of the mission house turned up nothing. Not wanting to worry Max, Vi told him to go to the schoolroom and watch over Gracie and Polly, so Mrs. O'Flaherty could help in the day nursery.

"Where's Lulu?" Max asked.

"I'll send her up to you," Vi replied vaguely. "I think the storm will be a strong one, but this house has withstood hurricanes, so there's no need for the girls to be afraid."

Max heard the tension in Miss Vi's voice and figured it was because of the coming storm. He ran off to tend to his sister and Polly.

Samaritan House was full of people. Mr. Gibbons and his workmen had gathered on the porch. There were a dozen children and several infants in the nursery, as well as the volunteers. The elderly ladies in the meeting room had been joined by more people, some of them clinic patients and others who sought safety in numbers at the mission.

Enoch and Rudy Hansen were going about the house, closing the interior shutters in all the rooms. There was always the danger that strong winds would hurl objects against the windows and break the glass. Vi found Enoch helping Dr. Bowman shutter the clinic.

"Has anyone seen Lulu?" she asked. "I can't find her, and I've accounted for everyone else."

Violet's Defiant Daughter

The doctor and Emily said they would join Vi's search, as Enoch would when he had secured the elevator. "We should look in every room, from the attic down," Dr. Bowman said with reassuring authority. "Don't worry, Vi. Say, could Mr. Gibbons and his men look around the grounds? Lulu might have slipped off to the stable or the shed."

Vi hurried to the porch and made her request. The telephone men were happy to search, and they scattered to check all the outbuildings. Not finding the little girl, they scoured the gardens; then Mr. Gibbons decided they should extend their search to the streets. He led a group into Wildwood Street, while three of his men took the side street.

Vi had to keep her rising anxiety in check. Panic would not help Lulu and might cause unnecessary stress for the guests at the mission. She went to the kitchen to tell Mary and Alma what was happening. Both women wanted to search, but Vi asked them to continue their work, preparing food and drinks for the people who were coming in.

Vi decided to check her office once more. That was where Lulu was supposed to be. Maybe there was some clue Vi had missed. The room had not changed since she'd come in earlier and closed the window, but she noticed something amiss. What was it? She looked around and realized that her desktop was clear, except for her eyeglasses. Then she saw Lulu's book on her chair, resting on a stack of receipts and business letters.

In an instant, Vi remembered: *I left Mark's letter on the desk! I was reading it again this morning, and Mr. Gibbons arrived, and I forgot to put the letter away. Could Lulu possibly have —?*

Her eyes darted about the room and alighted on something white in the corner behind the wastebasket. She grabbed up the crumpled pages, and her worst fears were confirmed.

"Dear Lord, what have I done?" she cried out. "My carelessness—how could I? To learn in this callous way—finding her father's letter—it would break her heart! Oh! The open window!"

Vi rushed from the office, across the kitchen, and out the back door. She ran around the side of the house to the patch of ground beneath the office window. Bending down, she clearly saw the imprints of two small boot heels in the soft, dry moss.

"She's run away," Vi said to herself. Fear overcame her, and she felt weak in every muscle of her body. "God, forgive me. It is all my fault. Tell me what to do to find her!"

CHAPTER

12

Searching and Finding

You are my hiding place...

PSALM 32:7

Searching and Finding

*T*hree men, coming through the mission's rear gate, saw young Miss Travilla kneeling on the ground beside the house. They hurried to her, and one of them called out, "We know which way she's gone!"

Vi looked in their direction. *What did the man say?* The fierce wind was drowning out all but the sounds of the storm.

The men came to her, and one put out his hand to help her rise. "We found an old fella boarding up his house, and he said he saw a blonde-headed girl out by herself maybe a half hour ago. He wasn't sure about the time. Stan here"—he motioned to one of his comrades—"went some ways along the dirt alleyway that winds back to the stores on Wildwood Street. I grew up in Wildwood, miss, so I know that alley bends around and comes out beside the Wildwood Hotel. Stan found this stuck between some rocks."

Stan was holding a dirty piece of ribbon. Vi took it and saw that it was pink silk grosgrain trimmed with pink lace. She herself had bought this ribbon as a present for Lulu.

"It's hers," she said softly, but the men understood her, despite the howling wind and repeated thunder.

"Then we know where to look," the first man said. "Stan, go find Mr. Gibbons and the other men. Miss Travilla, you get whoever's searching the house and tell 'em to meet us out front. That storm's about to break, and we need to get to them stores. I'm sure your little girl's there. Maybe someone took her in."

Violet's Defiant Daughter

As Stan rushed away, the third telephone man, who had not said anything, spoke up. "Don't you be too worried, ma'am. We'll have her back to you right soon."

"I'm going with you," Vi declared.

Before the man could tell her that it was too dangerous, Vi was gone.

Not five minutes later, she, Enoch, Dr. Bowman, and Rudy Hansen were gathered with Mr. Gibbons and his men on the mission porch. The rain had begun, and lightning streaked across the sky. The men all wore rain slickers, as did Vi. One of the men gave her an oilskin hat that covered her head and tied under her chin.

"Don't bother arguing with her!" Dr. Bowman shouted into Mr. Gibbons's ear. "It's a waste of precious time."

Mr. Gibbons shrugged with resignation.

On foot, the group of searchers, carrying oil lanterns, took to the streets. Their hastily devised strategy was to concentrate on the shopping area first, then widen their search if they didn't find Lulu. Despite the wind and rain, the men made good progress. Dr. Bowman stayed with Vi, who trailed just a little behind. When they reached the cluster of shops at the center of Wildwood, they began knocking on doors, asking if anyone had seen a young girl and getting permission to look in backyards and outbuildings. No one had seen Lulu, but several shopkeepers, including Mr. Hogg and his sons, joined the searchers. Hearing that Lulu was missing, Elwood had literally blanched; he was very fond of his employer's middle child. Recovering from his shock, Elwood suggested places to look, including hiding places where he'd played as a boy.

Seeing lights burning in the Wildwood Hotel, Vi and Dr. Bowman went there. To Vi's consternation, the hotel

owner—her old adversary, Tobias Clinch—was leaning against the front desk. Raucous voices and the music of a tinny piano came from the saloon.

Clinch didn't smile when he saw Vi and the doctor. Curling his lip, he said, "Look what the cat dragged in. A couple of drowned rats."

Vi would not let herself be baited. "We're not here to see you, Mr. Clinch. We're searching for a lost child. A girl, ten and a half years old and somewhat tall for her age. She has blonde hair in a braid, blue eyes, and freckles. She's wearing a pink dress."

"Oh, dear me," Clinch said in mocking concern. "Still tending the Lord's sheep are you, Miss Travilla?" Then his voice became hard. "No lost girls here."

"She might have sneaked in to escape the storm," Dr. Bowman said.

"Not likely," Clinch responded with a snort. "I've been right here for the last two hours. That worthless clerk of mine went off to see about his wife and kids. I've been stuck to this spot, and I've seen everybody who's come in that door. Till a minute ago, it was all men looking for a roof over their heads and a few stiff drinks."

"There are other doorways," Vi said in frustration.

"Let. . .me. . .think," Clinch said slowly, intending to annoy Vi as much as possible. "There's the cellar door, but it's bolted from the inside. The kitchen door? But my cook keeps it closed whenever the wind's up. The windows are all shuttered. Oh, there's my office door out back. Well, I keep it locked all the time, ever since that colored man of yours strong-armed his way in."

Vi ignored this remark. She didn't have any interest in discussing her last confrontation with Tobias Clinch.

Violet's Defiant Daughter

"Do we have your permission to search your grounds?" Dr. Bowman asked in a surprisingly calm tone.

Clinch rubbed his chin and cocked his head to one side and then the other. He pretended to be thinking over this request, for he enjoyed having an opportunity to tease these do-gooders from the mission.

Vi was ready to turn on her heel and resume the search without Clinch's permission when the man finally said, "Hunt around all you want. Just don't go agitating the horses in the stable. They're already spooked bad enough by the storm."

"I guess it's too much to ask for your help with the search," Dr. Bowman said.

Clinch was snarling when he replied, "You guess right, doc." Vi was already through the hotel door before these words left Clinch's mouth.

"I forgot about the stable!" Vi shouted to Dr. Bowman. "You check the cellar and the other doors. I don't trust Mr. Clinch's word. I'll go to the stable."

Fighting against the wind and rain, they entered the alley. Vi moved as fast as she could, though her steps were slowed by her sodden skirts, which felt plastered to her legs. Raising her lantern, she saw that the stable doors were securely battened. But there was a smaller door to the right, and it was loosely latched. Vi opened it and went in.

The lantern light penetrated only a couple of feet into the gloom, and Vi moved cautiously. She didn't see the small window until another flash of lightning made it visible. She realized that she was in the stable's tack area, which seemed a more likely place for Lulu to hide than near the horse stalls. Moving her light from side to side, she spotted the pile of feed bags—and two, bare, child-sized feet protruding from among them.

Lowering her lantern, Vi slipped out the little door again and scanned the darkness. Seeing a light coming toward her, she ran to Dr. Bowman. "I've found her!" she yelled in his ear. "Please, tell the men, so they can find shelter!"

The doctor nodded and disappeared into the raging gloom. Vi turned back to the stable.

Lulu had been preoccupied with thoughts about the house on College Street and Miss Moran and Kaki, and most of all, about Gracie and Max. She'd been wondering what they'd do without her and thinking that it wasn't fair for her to leave without them.

"I don't blame you for running away," a voice said. "I've come to ask you to forgive me for not being honest with you. Will you hear me out before you decide what to do?"

Lulu looked up to see Vi standing a few feet away, holding a light.

"You lied to me," Lulu said in a hard, cold tone. "*You and Papa.*"

"I know," Vi replied. "We didn't intend to hurt you or to be dishonest, but you're right, Lulu. It was lying by omission, and I understand now how wrong we were."

"Then why'd you do it?" Lulu demanded. "Why didn't you just tell us you were going to get married?"

"Because we thought that you and Gracie and Max should have a chance to get to know me first," Vi said plainly, "before any final decision was made."

Violet's Defiant Daughter

"But you did decide, didn't you?" Lulu said in a breaking voice. "It was in Papa's letter. About a wedding! That's decided!"

"Did you read the whole letter?" Vi asked.

Defiantly, Lulu declared, "No, but I read enough! I saw those words—*marriage* and *wedding*. And I read what he wrote about you being husband and wife. I thought you were my friend, but you lied to me. You were just trying to make me and Max and Gracie love you, so you could marry our Papa! Then you wouldn't have to be our friend anymore. You'd have Papa, and you wouldn't have to care about us anymore. You won't care about Samaritan House either. You'll just leave all those people to take care of themselves!"

Now that Lulu's fears and anger were finally coming out, it was like a dam breaking—a great flood of words and feelings. It didn't all make sense, but Vi understood. It had happened to her after her father died and she had felt such a burden of guilt and shame. She had kept her feelings inside for months, until one afternoon in a dark, cold attic at Ion, her mother had found her hiding. Vi had poured out her feelings in a great rush of emotion. Vi knew that, like her younger self, Lulu had to give vent to all the feelings bottled up inside.

Lulu was sitting up straight now, grasping the burlap bags as if to steady herself.

"Why'd you have to do it, Miss Vi?" Lulu raged, tears streaming down her face. "Why'd you have to make Papa love you? Why do you want Papa to forget our mother?"

"I don't," Vi said simply.

"But if he marries you, he'll forget all about her, and then he'll forget about loving us, and all he'll care about is you—making *you* happy!"

Searching and Finding

Lulu bent sideways and buried her face against one of the feed bags.

"I thought I could—could save our family—if I made you go away," she said between sobs. "I couldn't save my Mamma, but I thought I could save our family—keep us together if—if I made you hate me. If I was really bad, then you'd hate me and not want to be our stepmother. That's why I played the trick with the frogs, and I was gonna do a lot worse. Then you forgave me, and you were like a real friend, and I couldn't do it. I wanted to be your friend. I never had a real friend before, 'cept Max and Gracie."

Vi set the lantern on the hard-packed dirt floor and came to sit on a grain bag beside Lulu, but she didn't touch the sobbing child.

"Friends make mistakes. I made a very big one when I decided to keep the truth about my feelings for your father from you," Vi said, keeping her voice steady. "But I am your friend, and I always will be. I may never be your stepmother, but I will always be your friend."

"What do you mean—about never being my stepmother?" Lulu asked in a small voice. She didn't raise her head, but she managed a peek at Vi. In the lantern light, Vi's face looked very beautiful and very sad. Lulu saw Vi close her eyes tightly for a moment, and she was sure Vi was saying a prayer.

Then Vi said, "Lulu, I am going to tell you the whole truth, from my heart. I love your father. Maybe I loved him from the first day I saw him. I don't know, but what I feel for him is the truest feeling I have ever had for another person. One of the reasons I love him so much is that he loves you and Max and Gracie so deeply. He would do anything for you. Those years you lived with your Aunt Gert, your

Papa thought he was doing the right thing. His grief after the death of your dear mother was so great that he thought his sadness would hurt his children."

Lulu raised her head a little and said, "I thought it was because we reminded him of Mamma. I thought it hurt him to see us and to think of her."

"It may have, a bit at first. But he stayed away because he thought you would be happier without him," Vi explained. "When he discovered how wrong he was, he did everything he could to make it up to you three. And you and your brother and sister brought love to his life again."

"We did?" Lulu was curious now, and she sat up again.

"All of us who care about your Papa saw what was happening," Vi continued. "I don't think he realized how he was changing at first. But I could read it in his letters. You know that he was writing to me when you were living in Kingstown, don't you?"

"Oh, sure. He told us all about you. That's when I started thinking you might be trying to marry him," Lulu said in her matter-of-fact tone.

A little laugh escaped Vi, and she said, "You always amaze me, young lady. At any rate, you three made him understand how important it is to love and be loved. You gave him a great gift, Lulu, by reminding him that the human heart has a limitless capacity for love. It was because of his love for you that he was able to express himself to me, and I knew I loved his three children long before I ever laid eyes on you.

"But I promised you the entire truth," Vi went on. "I was a little afraid of you, too. I knew—and your Papa knew—that we would never do anything to harm you. That means, Lulu, that there will be no marriage unless you agree to it. I will not wed your father if our marriage will cause you pain. That's why we didn't tell you our plans. Our hope was that you and Gracie and Max could get to know me and trust me without the pressure of thinking you had to please Mark—your Papa. I wanted to have this summer to build a good and trusting relationship with you. But I let you down, Lulu, and I'll understand if you can't trust me now."

Vi fell silent, and Lulu thought for some time. Then she said, "You really wouldn't marry Papa if we—if *I* said 'no'?"

"I wouldn't," Vi said. "You said you wanted a real friend, and that's what I want. I want to be your real and true friend. Friends can't resent and distrust one another. If I marry your Papa against your wishes, then your resentment might grow and affect your feelings for your Papa. I can't let that happen. Everything might be all right, but I can't risk the happiness of four people I love so very much."

"Papa would be so mad at me if I messed things up," Lulu said.

"No, he wouldn't," Vi said firmly. "If you had read all his letter, you'd know that he wrote of this very thing. You three are his reason for being, and he would never be angry with you because of your feelings. His hope is that his children will welcome me into the family, but if you can't, he understands. He really and truly understands."

"If you and Papa *did* get married," Lulu said with care, "would he forget our Mamma? Would we have to call you 'Mamma' and never speak of her again?"

"Of course not," Vi said. "I don't ever want you or your father to forget your mother and how much she loved you. She will always be part of you, and you must cherish her memory. In my memory, my own Papa is as alive to me as

ever, though he is with our Father in Heaven. I didn't know your mother, but in the love that you and Max and Gracie have for her, I can see what a fine person she was. No one can ever take her place in your heart, Lulu, and we would never ask that of you.

"Lulu, if I *did* marry your Papa, I would be your step-mother, and I would be responsible for you as if I were your mother. But I wouldn't be your mother. Have you ever known anyone who has a stepmother?"

"No," Lulu admitted. "But I've read all about them. In stories, stepmothers are always mean and treat their stepchildren terribly. And they always love their own children better."

"Some stepparents may be like the ones in your stories," Vi conceded, "but in my experience, they are good and caring people who love their stepchildren without distinction. And you do know someone who has a stepmother. You know *my* mother. My Grandmamma Rose is her step-mother. Do they seem like the stepfamilies in your stories?"

"Not at all," Lulu said. She thought perhaps she had heard this news before, but a flicker of doubt made her say, "I guess your mother was just a baby when it happened. Everybody loves babies."

"My mother was eleven, a year older than you are now, when my grandfather married my Grandmamma Rose," Vi replied. "You see, Lulu, children are God's gift to parents, but not to parents alone. Do you remember, in the Gospel of Matthew, when people brought their children to see Jesus, and the disciples wanted to send the children away? But Jesus said, 'Let the little children come to me, and do not hinder them, for the kingdom of heaven belongs to such as these.' Jesus loves all children, and His model is ours to follow. My

Grandmamma Rose loves my mother just the same as she loves my aunt and uncle, who are her own children. Jesus tells us to love every child. He says, 'For whoever welcomes a child like this in my name welcomes me.' "

"Is that true? Does Jesus love all children? Even bad ones?" Lulu asked.

"Yes, I believe He does," Vi said. "Jesus is not a fair-weather friend. He loves us when we are being good, and He loves us when we're naughty or thoughtless—even though He may not like our behavior. Jesus is compassionate and merciful toward our human weaknesses. I think perhaps He loves us most when we admit our weaknesses and realize how much we need Him. He knows and understands everything in our hearts, even our deepest doubts and confusions.

"Lulu, I'm sorry for not being honest with you from the start. I want you to return to the mission with me, for my first responsibility is to see that you are safe and restored to your family."

"Does everybody know that I ran away?" Lulu asked fearfully. "Do Max and Gracie know?"

"The adults know that you were missing, and they are very worried about you. I asked Mrs. O'Flaherty to stay with Max and Gracie and to answer their questions. But I think it is up to you to tell your brother and sister what happened, in your own way. Jesus will help you say what is in your heart, if you let Him."

"I'm glad He knows what's in my heart," Lulu sighed, "because I'm not sure I do. I'm sorry I ran off, Miss Vi. I didn't think."

"And I didn't think when I left your father's letter on my desk," Vi said. "But I believe the Lord wanted us to have

this conversation. He has taught me that I cannot control another person's feelings. If I'd been honest with you from the start, you may not have loved me or even liked me, but you would trust me."

"I trust you," Lulu said quickly. "I know you and Papa thought you were doing the best thing. I guess we all made big mistakes. I guess I've got lots to talk to Jesus about."

"Me too," Vi said.

"Will you talk to me some more, Miss Vi?" Lulu asked. "I've got some stuff to figure out."

"We can talk as often as you like," Vi said.

⁓

Dr. Bowman had told all the searchers that the lost lamb was found. He thanked the men and said that he would escort Miss Travilla and young Lulu back to Samaritan House. The telephone men and shopkeepers were greatly relieved that the day had not ended in tragedy, and they shook hands all around before going their separate ways. Mr. Gibbons promised to deliver the good news to Mrs. O'Flaherty at the mission and said he and his men would return the next day to finish their work.

The storm was abating, and the wind was calmer. But the rain continued to fall for a while, and Elwood Hogg was glad of it. The rain drops masked the tears he shed when he learned that young Lulu was safe. He said he would bring the carriage right away.

"There's no rush, Elwood," Dr. Bowman replied. He laid his arm around the young man's shoulder and said, "I believe that Lulu and Miss Vi have a good deal to talk about. You go home and see your mother before you get the carriage. Give her a kiss and tell her you love her. Families need tending, Elwood, just like gardens."

Dr. Bowman strolled off toward the stable, where he would await Vi and Lulu.

Elwood thought about Lulu and what might have happened if Miss Vi hadn't found her. He thought about his own ma, and how she tended to him and his brothers, without ever expecting thanks. Elwood turned toward his home, above the butcher's shop, to follow Dr. Bowman's advice.

CHAPTER

A Golden Occasion

Her children arise and call her blessed...

PROVERBS 31:28

A Golden Occasion

*M*iss Moran was so relieved to see the children that she didn't immediately notice Lulu's badly soiled dress, muddy boots, and torn stockings. When she did take note of the girl's condition, Vi explained, "Lulu got caught outside in the storm and took shelter in a stable. Dr. Bowman has checked her over, and except for a scrape on her knee, no harm was done. The doctor has prescribed a hot bath. That's all."

Gracie and Max were very curious about Lulu's adventure, but knew their sister would tell them what had happened—when she was ready.

"I'll take you right up to your room, Lulu, and get you out of those filthy clothes," Miss Moran said in her motherly way.

"Can Miss Vi take me?" Lulu asked.

"Why, sure," Miss Moran smiled. "Miss Vi can get you undressed while I run your bath water. I know just how you like it."

Vi didn't show her surprise at Lulu's request, but she felt a flush of happiness when Lulu took her hand and said, "Will you help me, Miss Vi?"

They went upstairs to Lulu's pretty bedroom with the butterfly wallpaper. Neither of them spoke at first. Vi knelt down to unlace Lulu's boots, and then she stood to assist the child out of her damp dress and into her cozy robe and slippers.

Finally Lulu said, "I know that you didn't mean to deceive me, Miss Vi. I guess there are things that mothers and fathers don't always tell their children, and that's okay."

"There are decisions that parents must make for their children, and you're right, Lulu, parents don't always discuss those decisions with their children at first," Vi replied.

"Like Papa sending us to Miss Broadbent's school," Lulu said as she undid her braid. "Papa made that decision, and I bet he talked to you about it, didn't he?"

"Yes, he asked me to recommend a good school for you and Gracie, and I said I thought you'd like Miss Broadbent's. Was I wrong?"

"No, ma'am. Not at all," Lulu said quickly. "But I was just thinking that I'd never have picked Miss Broadbent's all by myself. If it had been up to me, we'd have stayed in Kingstown. But I'm glad we came here, and it's good that you helped Papa make those decisions. I guess maybe Papa really does need you, 'cause you are his best friend."

Vi didn't reply, for she didn't know what to say. She got Lulu's brush from the dresser and began to smooth the girl's tangled locks.

"You're good at brushing," Lulu said after a time. "I remember my Mamma brushing my hair. I remember things like that—how she touched my hair and how she always sang a lullaby to Gracie to get her to sleep. Today, when you said that about Jesus loving the children, I remembered my Mamma telling us the same thing."

Lulu turned around suddenly and looked at Vi with an expression of complete openness. "Why did God take her from us, Miss Vi? Why did he take your Papa from you?"

Vi sat down on Lulu's bed and put her arm around the child's waist. "I don't have the answer to that," she said. "There are things in this life that we must trust to God when we have no clear answers. But I do know that God is good all of the time, and He loves us completely. He gives

us our time in this life, and when our lives here are over, God's children can go to Heaven and be with Him forever. Can you imagine it, Lulu, to be loved forever? To be free of every sorrow and healed of every pain by God's love for us? There can be no greater joy."

"Some people told us that when Mamma died," Lulu said, "but I didn't understand. How could we feel joy when we'd never see our Mamma again?"

"It is hard to understand," Vi said in agreement. "But if we really believe in our Lord's promise to us, we know that death is not the end of our journey and we will be reunited with our loved ones later, when we go to be with God. It's the beginning of the most glorious part of our existence, when our Heavenly Father folds us in His arms forever."

"I know Mamma is happy there, in His arms," Lulu said with a little sniff. She snuggled closer to Vi and went on, "Do you think she still loves us?"

"Oh, I know she does!" Vi said. "Loving doesn't stop because we are apart. Your Papa has been away in Mexico for almost six weeks. Yet do you love him any less?"

"I think I love him even more when he's away," Lulu replied. "I guess that's 'cause I miss him so much. Sometimes I'm scared he won't come back."

"Do you feel that way now?" Vi asked.

Lulu considered for some moments, and her thoughts surprised her. "No, I don't," she said, looking up so that Vi saw the amazed look in her teary eyes.

"All the time he's been gone, I haven't worried that he wouldn't come back," Lulu said. "It's so strange. Before, when he'd visit us in Boston, I was always afraid he'd get sick, like Mamma did, or something bad would happen to him, and I'd never see him again."

Violet's Defiant Daughter

Vi said with a loving smile. "It's possible, isn't it, that without realizing it, you have come to trust your father's love completely. Maybe now you know that his love for you and Max and Gracie is so strong that you will never lose it. Whether he is here with you or far away, you children are always in his heart."

"And you're in his heart, too, Miss Vi," Lulu said shyly. "Even if you went away and Papa never saw you again, he'd keep on loving you. If I'd made you so mad at me that you wouldn't be my stepmother, Papa'd still love you, and he'd love me even if I caused him to be sad."

Lulu looked down and said so softly that Vi had to lean close to hear her, "I guess it would be a good thing. . . if you marry my Papa. I guess he's got more than enough love for all of us. I guess—" She paused, and then she lifted her head up and exclaimed, "I know that I'd like you to be my stepmother!"

Lulu's words brought a physical thrill to Vi. She could literally feel happiness flood through her, and instinctively she drew Lulu closer. "Are you sure, darling?" she asked. "Are you very sure?"

"I'm sure," Lulu said with a firmness that was no longer defiant.

~

The next day, Lulu told her brother and sister everything that had happened during the storm and what she and Vi had discussed. She did not leave out anything.

When she finished, Max declared, "You are the stubbornest girl I ever saw, Lulu! You're just like an old mule when you get some idea in your head. Sometimes that's good—but, oh boy, not this time."

"But you're happy now, aren't you? Happy about Papa and Miss Vi?" Gracie asked, her small face frowning with concern.

"Really happy," Lulu assured her. "I think we're gonna have just about the best stepmother in the world."

"It took you long enough to figure that out," Max retorted. For some time, both he and Gracie had been sure that their father planned to marry Miss Vi, so they were not surprised when Lulu told them of the engagement. But Max wasn't quite ready to let Lulu off the hook. "You should have known Papa would only marry somebody real special, like Mamma," he said.

"I know that now," Lulu said in an apologetic way. "I really do, Max. And I'm sorry for everything I did. I ought to have talked to you. I wish I had."

A smile replacing her frown, Gracie said, "Tell Lulu you forgive her, Max."

At last, Max smiled. " 'Course I forgive you, Lulu. Say, are you gonna tell Papa what you did?"

"I am," Lulu replied. "Miss Vi said I should tell him myself, and I will, as soon as he gets home."

The children were in Gracie's bedroom, and Gracie had been sitting in her little rocking chair. Now she jumped up, ran to her sister, and tightly hugged Lulu's waist. "Papa won't be mad at you," Gracie said. "He'll understand. I know he will."

"Yeah, that's right," Max agreed. "And it's all worked out for the best, between you and Miss Vi. That'll make Papa real glad, and us too."

Gracie loosened her hold on Lulu and began skipping around the room. "We're going to have a wedding!" she sang in a funny, cheerful tune.

"Say, what should we call Miss Vi after she and Papa get married?" Max asked.

"Miss Vi said that we should decide," Lulu answered, for she had asked Vi the very same question the night before. "She said she'll be happy with whatever we want. Oh! There's something else. She wanted to know if we could keep her and Papa's engagement a secret till Papa gets home. Miss Vi said it's a good kind of secret, and everybody will know just as soon as Papa gets back."

"We've got a 'portant secret!" Gracie sang, resuming her skipping dance.

"Hush," Max laughed. "It won't be a secret for long if you keep on singing like that."

Gracie giggled. Then in a tiny musical whisper, she sang, "I can keep a secret. A very happy secret."

The visit to Ion, for Elsie Travilla's birthday party, began on the following Thursday. Ed came into the city to get Vi, Mrs. O'Flaherty, and the Raymond children. They were a very cheerful group as the large carriage rocked along the country road to the Travilla estate.

"What are you giving your mother for her birthday?" Max asked Ed.

"I can't tell, but it's going to be a very special surprise," Ed said with a wide grin. "Maybe the best surprise Mamma's ever had."

Vi had already tried, several times, to coax the secret from her big brother, but Ed would not give her so much as a hint. All he would say was that the present was better than gold.

A Golden Occasion

When they reached the main house at Ion, Rosemary, Danny, and Tansy and Marigold Evans were waiting under the portico. After greeting her sister and Mrs. O'Flaherty, Rosemary said excitedly to the young Raymonds, "Mamma has made us your hosts, and we're going to have ever so much fun. As soon as you've unpacked, we're going down to the lake and have a boat ride. Maybe we can fish, and then we're having a picnic supper. Don't worry, Vi. Ben and Crystal would be with us the whole time."

The children's group grew larger the next day, when Vi's aunt, Rosie Dinsmore Lacey, arrived with her youngsters. Vi hardly saw the young people on Friday and Saturday, for they were always dashing off to some new activity—horseback rides, swimming in the cool lake, a hayride, baseball games. When there was a lull, the girls went to the creek not far from the house.

Thanks to the big storm, the water in the creek was high enough for wading. They'd walk barefoot in the gentle current and squish their toes in the mud along the water's edge. There was a big willow tree that overhung the creek, and the girls would laze under its dangling boughs and tell each other stories. Mary Lacey, a small, gentle girl of fifteen, had a particularly vivid imagination, and her recounting of the legends of King Arthur and the Knights of the Round Table kept everyone, including Gracie and Marigold, enraptured. The girls also talked about their families. When Rosemary entertained them with the story of the time her twin brothers had played a mean trick on her and Vi with a giant bullfrog (in Rosemary's memory, the frog loomed as large as a bear), Lulu laughed as hard as she had when Vi first told the tale.

Lulu controlled the temptation to reveal the secret about her father and Vi, but it occurred to her that when her Papa married, all these children would be her family, including Tansy and Marigold, who had been adopted by Mrs. Travilla. In all the time Lulu had plotted against Vi, it hadn't occurred to her that all these kind and friendly people might become her stepfamily. *You really can be silly sometimes, Lulu Raymond*, she told herself when this realization finally dawned on her.

Vi's brothers Harold and Herbert returned from their university on Saturday morning, and Lulu thought that this might be Ed Travilla's secret present, until Mrs. O'Flaherty explained that the twins' visit had been planned for some time.

When the party began late Saturday afternoon, the Raymond children — dressed in their best party clothes — were introduced to so many members of the Dinsmore family that Lulu gave up trying to remember all their names. She confided her difficulty to Rosemary, and the older girl laughed merrily, "You're just like Vi. She always had the hardest time with people's names." Lulu was pleased by the comparison to Miss Vi.

Vi made a special point of introducing the children to Mr. and Mrs. Louis Embery, Dr. Dick Percival, and Reverend and Mrs. James Keith, who had come up from Louisiana and were staying at Vi's great-grandfather's home at Roselands.

After a while, Lulu realized that Ed Travilla was nowhere to be seen. She hadn't seen him all day, not even at breakfast. Where could he be? And what was the present he had for his mother? She wandered away from the garden, where all the guests were gathered, and into the house. She peeked into the front parlor, which had been opened onto the dining room, creating a huge single room. The mantels and every table were banked with large arrangements of multi-hued flowers. The cool fragrance of roses filled the air. The long, rectangular dining table was draped in a white lace cloth and set with beautiful china, silver, and tall crystal glasses, which sparkled in the light streaming through the tall, open windows. Remembering Mary Lacey's stories about King Arthur and Camelot, Lulu imagined that his castle might have looked as beautiful as this.

She was thinking about castles when she heard a deep voice. She looked around the room and the hallway, but she saw no one.

"They're here, but that's not what I want to say to you," the voice said loudly. It seemed to come from the library or maybe the sitting room. Lulu couldn't make out who was speaking, but he sounded angry.

"What do you mean, you're going to take a job?" the voice demanded.

Another voice cut in. Lulu couldn't distinguish the words, but she thought a woman was speaking.

Then the man said, "But you can't marry anybody if you're teaching!"

The other voice said something, and then the man said, "You must know how I feel. I can't live without. . ."

His voice softened, and Lulu couldn't hear the rest of what he said. But in a flash, she knew that the man was Ed Travilla. When he was shouting, she hadn't realized who it was; she had never seen Vi's charming brother in a temper. But in those final few words, he sounded like himself.

Lulu was totally bewildered by what she'd heard. Who was he talking to? Lulu couldn't guess. But she knew that she shouldn't be listening, so she hurried back to the party. Mrs. O'Flaherty saw the anxious look on the child's face and asked, "Are you all right? I haven't seen you scowling like that in some days."

"It's just the light in my eyes," Lulu said. And it was true. The lowering sun had struck her face as she left the house and caused her to blink in discomfort.

Mrs. O took Lulu's hand and said, "I'm going to talk to Mrs. Embery. She is Vi's cousin Molly—Molly Percival before she married. She's a famous writer, and one of the nicest, most interesting young women I've ever known. Did you see that she walks with a cane?"

Lulu nodded.

"Well, she had a terrible accident when she was a girl, and for many years she couldn't walk at all. But with God's mercy and the help of her brother, Dr. Percival, and her husband, she has recovered much of her mobility. It has taken great courage on her part. Now she's writing a book about her experience. Would you like to come with me and talk to her?"

Intrigued by what Mrs. O'Flaherty told her, Lulu forgot about the angry words she'd overheard just minutes before. Mrs. Molly Percival Embery proved to be even nicer and more interesting than Mrs. O'Flaherty had said. Lulu was so intent on their conversation that she didn't see Ed Travilla come out of the house, accompanied by Zoe Love. Nor did she see when Ed searched out his grandfather, Horace Dinsmore, Jr.—who was also Zoe's guardian. Ed and Mr. Dinsmore, both with grave expressions, retreated into the house, but Lulu didn't see that either. Her attention was fully engaged until a bell rang and Mr. Embery appeared to help his wife and escort her, Mrs. O, and Lulu to supper.

The buffet meal was wonderful. Lulu joined Rosemary, Gracie, and the other girls, who took their plates out to the veranda.

"Will there be a birthday cake?" Gracie asked.

"A huge one," Rosemary said. "Crystal decorated it herself, with sugar flowers and Mamma's initials in real gold letters. Mamma hasn't seen it, but I have, and it's almost too pretty to eat!"

"But you will force yourself to have a piece," said Mary Lacey with a sly grin.

"Only a tiny slice, if I absolutely must," Rosemary sighed dramatically.

This got a big laugh. Everybody, even Lulu and Gracie, knew about Rosemary's fondness for desserts, the richer the better.

After supper, the children joined the adult guests in the parlor to await the birthday speeches and the cake. Elsie was seated near the dining table and beside her sat an elderly black woman — Aunt Chloe, who was Elsie's oldest and dearest friend. Reverend Keith spoke first and offered a prayer. Then Cal Conley extended birthday wishes from everyone at Roselands. Molly Embery, supported on her husband's arm, gave a lovely speech on the theme of God's gift of life and her cousin Elsie's gift for transforming each day into an adventure of the spirit. Most of the guests expected Trip Dinsmore, Elsie's brother, to speak next, but Trip had given his time to his father.

"For half of a century, you have graced my life and blessed my days," Horace Dinsmore began, looking at Elsie. "I had a speech prepared, but instead of my own poor words, I have been given the honor of bestowing a wonderful gift."

He motioned to someone at the side of the room and Zoe walked to his side.

"As most of you know, Zoe came into our home and hearts four years ago. My wife and I have watched her grow from a girl to a splendid young woman, and I have had the privilege of being her teacher as well as her guardian. Now her education is over, and I'm pleased to announce that in just a few weeks, our Zoe will become Miss Love, skilled instructress in Latin and French at Miss Broadbent's Female Academy."

There was a round of applause, though most people were wondering what this announcement had to do with Elsie's birthday.

Mr. Dinsmore raised a hand for silence. "At the end of her year at Miss Broadbent's, Zoe will be returning to us to begin another career. This day, I have had the great honor to give my permission for dear Zoe to become the wife of. . ."

He waved, and someone walked forward, but Lulu couldn't see what was happening until Ed, beaming with happiness, stood next to Zoe. Mr. Dinsmore smiled almost as broadly and said, "The wife of this besotted young man, my grandson Edward."

He placed Zoe's hand in Ed's, and the guests erupted in clapping, cheering, and laughter. Elsie embraced the couple, saying, "I was beginning to think you two would never get to this day. I am so incredibly happy for you both."

"A year is a long time," Ed said, hugging his mother, "but Papa waited that long for you. I know what teaching means to Zoe, but I couldn't let her move to India Bay unless I had her promise."

"I hope you aren't upset at this surprise," Zoe said, as Elsie kissed her.

"Upset? I couldn't have asked for better from either of you," Elsie replied, crying happy tears. "Oh, my darling Zoe, my dear, darling daughter."

Guests began pressing forward to congratulate the couple, but Ed lifted his arms, and once again the room grew still. "Some of you are aware that I was planning a special surprise for Mamma," he said, "but believe it or not, this isn't it! Until today, when Zoe accepted my proposal, I had nearly resigned myself to a life of lonely bachelorhood. I have another gift for you, Mamma—one you have wanted for a long time."

Ed put his arm around Elsie's waist and turned her toward the door that led from the pantry into the dining room. A man and a woman entered. The man was holding a child of about three years. The woman, who looked as much like Elsie as a photograph, ran a few steps and nearly fell into Elsie's arm.

"We're home, Mamma. Home for good," Missy Travilla Leland sobbed.

Yes, Ed had given his mother a present better than gold, better than all the riches in the world. Her eldest child—her firstborn—was home again, returned from Rome with her husband, Lester, and their son.

"Can it be true?" Elsie said, stroking Missy's face with her hand, as if she could only believe what she touched. "Home for good?"

"Yes, Mamma," Missy replied through her tears, "it's true. Really, really true."

Elsie now embraced Lester and the grandson she'd only seen once before, when he was an infant. The little boy slipped easily into his grandmother's arms.

There was much talking and quite a few tears were shed among the guests when Horace Dinsmore spoke again.

Violet's Defiant Daughter

"I'm sure you will excuse my daughter and the rest of our Travilla family for a little while. But please, do not leave, for we have a cake to cut. In the meantime, refresh yourselves and enjoy the music that Mrs. Maurene O'Flaherty has agreed to play for us."

Vi had been too stunned by Missy's appearance to move. But when her mother and sister left the dining room, Vi went quickly to catch up with them. She was slowed by well-wishers but finally made her way into the hall. Before she'd gone two steps, however, Ben came out of the library and stood in front of her.

"There's a man to see you," he said.

"Oh, not now," Vi said in exasperation. "I have to see Missy."

"The man says it's urgent, Miss Vi. He's come a long way to get here. He rode it at a gallop, and he's covered in dust and dirt. I think you oughta see him right now."

Vi hesitated. *Perhaps something has happened at the mission. Someone may be injured. Or a fire!*

"Tell Missy and Mamma I'm coming," she said to Ben. Then she swung open the library door and entered.

The man was standing by the window at the opposite of the room, his back to her. But Vi instantly recognized him.

"Mark!" she cried out, and she ran into his open arms.

A quarter of an hour later, Vi returned to the parlor. The guests assumed that her glowing face and sparkling eyes

were the result of her reunion with her sister, brother-in-law, and young nephew. The room was bursting with good-will, and all the guests wanted to know if the Lelands were back for good and how long they would be staying at Ion. Vi, who still hadn't seen her sister, was briskly polite to one and all, but her eyes roamed the room in search of three children. First, she found Gracie, who was sitting with Tansy, Marigold, and Aunt Chloe. Next, she located Max, standing with a group of the boys around the piano. Vi managed to catch his eye and gestured to him.

Where can Lulu be? she wondered. Then she heard the unmistakable laughter of young girls. It came from a cor-ner, but a cluster of older ladies blocked her view. Taking Max and Gracie by their hands, Vi led them toward the cor-ner and saw Lulu sitting on the window ledge. Vi intended to approach Lulu decorously, but Max called out, "Lulu, come on! Miss Vi needs us."

Mark was standing close to the library door when Vi opened it, so almost at the moment they saw him, his three children were in his arms. They hugged and laughed, and Gracie tugged at her Papa's new, shaggy beard.

"You came home all scratchy," the littlest Raymond giggled.

"Are those your jungle clothes?" Lulu questioned. "They smell kinda strange."

"Did you find the ancient city?" Max asked with excite-ment.

Mark sat down on the couch, and the children gathered around him.

"The beard is scratchy, Gracie, my pet, and I will shave it as soon as I find a good, sharp razor," he said, caressing the little girl's head.

Turning to Lulu, he said, "These are my jungle clothes. I was so anxious to get back that I didn't unpack my trunk to get my city clothes. I will give my clothing and myself a good wash—even if I have to jump into the Travillas' lake."

To Max he said, "We didn't find the city, but we found evidence of it. I have drawings of what we discovered, but I left them with my luggage at our house."

"How'd you get here, Papa?" Lulu asked. "We weren't expecting you till Monday."

"We returned to Mexico City a few days ahead of plan, and once I read your letters, I decided to leave early. I got to India Bay by train and boat, but when I reached College Street, Miss Moran told me you were all here. I couldn't wait to see you, could I?"

"Oh, no, Papa," Gracie said gravely, "and we couldn't wait *that* long to see *you*."

"I rented a swift horse at the livery stable, and here I am," Mark said. "I hope I haven't spoiled your party," he added, looking at Vi.

"Oh, Papa, such nice things have happened," Gracie said. "Mr. Ed is going to marry Miss Zoe, and Miss Vi's big sister has come home from Italy. Miss Zoe's going to be a teacher at our new school, before she gets married."

"That all happened tonight!' Max exclaimed. "We've got lots more to tell you 'bout the rest of the summer. You won't believe all that we've done."

Gracie placed her hand on her Papa's cheek and said, "And you and Miss Vi are getting married."

This remark astounded Mark, and he looked at Vi with a puzzled expression. She gave a little shrug of her shoulders

and smiled. "Your children are very clever, Professor Raymond, at uncovering secrets."

"Well, what do you think?" Mark asked his children, though he wasn't altogether certain he wanted to hear their answer. He looked at Lulu and said, "Tell me your thoughts, my darling."

"I think. . . " Lulu began. She stopped, wanting to use the right words. Then she started again, slowly. "I think you should get married because you love Miss Vi, and she loves you, and she loves us too. Papa, she's been a real, true friend all the time you've been away, and she's taught me a lot about what love means. And—and—we all love her, and we want you to get married, so she can be our new mother."

Mark stared at his middle child.

"I mean it, Papa!" Lulu went on. "We've all got a whole lot of room in our hearts for love. Miss Vi taught me that. She taught me how our hearts have a"—she looked up at Vi and smiled—"a *limitless capacity* for love. We can still love our Mamma who's with God, and we can love our new Mamma who's right here for us all the time."

"Your new Mamma?" Mark said in a hushed tone.

"That's what we decided we want to call Miss Vi," Max said.

"We thought it out together," Gracie explained.

"We want Miss Vi to be our Mamma," Lulu said. "And Gracie and me will be her daughters, and Max will be her son. We'll be a family!"

Mark stretched out his long arms and drew his youngsters close. In a choked voice, he said, "That's what I want too. Thank you, children."

They nestled against him for several moments. Then Lulu declared, "Papa, you gotta hug Miss Vi. She's family now. Almost. When are you getting married anyway? Miss Zoe and Mr. Ed are waiting a year, but I think that's too long."

"Far too long," Mark said. He strengthened his hold on the children for a moment, and then he rose from the couch.

"How long does it take to plan a wedding?" he asked, extending his hand to Vi.

"Not too long," Vi said, placing her hand on his. Mark pulled her into a warm hug. The children clustered around, and Mark drew them into the hug.

Tears of joy were rolling down Vi's cheeks. This was her family now: her beloved professor, pure-hearted Max, gentle and loving little Gracie, and Lulu. Vi smiled to herself. *My dear, defiant daughter*, she thought. *We've had quite an adventure this summer, and I'm sure it won't be the last we will share. You've let me into your heart, Lulu, and you've taught me a great lesson about trust. Thank you, darling daughter. With God's help, I will never let you down again.*

The children began chattering with excitement, and Gracie asked, "Can we tell now, Papa? Can we tell everybody about you and Miss Vi?"

Before Mark could reply, Lulu said, "Not now, Gracie. The party and everything is for Mrs. Travilla's birthday. It should be her special night, don't you think?" she added, looking at Vi.

"That's really thoughtful of you, Lulu," Vi said with a proud smile.

Mark swung Gracie off the floor and said, "Can you keep our secret for another day?"

"If I have to, Papa," Gracie said, with only a small hint of disappointment.

A Golden Occasion

There was a knock at the library door, and Ben entered. "I have a bath ready for you, Professor, and some of Mr. Ed's clean clothes that I know will fit. I put you in the guest room next to the children. Miss Vi, your big sister's about to bust her buttons to see you, and your mother says to bring these young 'uns into the dining room, so she can cut Crystal's beautiful cake."

"Do you mind if I clean up before I join you?" Mark asked his fiancée and his children.

The children released him, and Vi said, "Take your time, Mark. I'm sure the party will go on for quite a while."

Mark followed Ben out of the room, with Vi and the youngsters just behind. Gracie skipped ahead, and Vi felt a hand slip into hers — Lulu's hand. It felt so natural, so good, and at long last, so very, very right.

What hidden dangers lurk on a tropical island?
Can Vi discover the truth in time?
Or will a masked villain destroy her new happiness?

Violet's story continues in:

VIOLET'S FOREIGN INTRIGUE

Book Eight
of the
*A Life of Faith:
Violet Travilla* Series

MCP
Mission City Press

For more information, write to

Mission City Press at 202 Second Ave. South
Franklin, Tennessee 37064
or visit our Web Site at:

www.alifeoffaith.com

Collect all of our Elsie products!

A Life of Faith: Elsie Dinsmore Series

* Now Available as a Dramatized Audiobook!

Collect all of our Millie products!

A Life of Faith: Millie Keith Series

* Now Available as a Dramatized Audiobook!

Beloved Literary Characters
Come to Life!

*Y*our favorite heroines, Millie Keith, Elsie Dinsmore, Violet Travilla, and Laylie Colbert are now available as lovely designer dolls from Mission City Press.

*M*ade of soft-molded vinyl, these beautiful, fully-jointed 18¾" dolls come dressed in historically-accurate clothing and accessories. They wonderfully reflect the Biblical virtues that readers have come to know and love about Millie, Elsie, Violet, and Laylie.

For more information, visit www.alifeoffaith.com or check with your local Christian retailer.

A Life of Faith® Products from Mission City Press —

"It's Like Having a Best Friend From Another Time"

A LIFE OF FAITH®
Girls Club

An Imaginative New Approach to Faith Education

Imagine…an easy way to gather the young girls in your community for fun, fellowship, and faith-inspiring lessons that will further their personal relationship with our Lord, Jesus Christ. Now you can, simply by hosting an A Life of Faith Girls Club.

This popular Girls Club was created to teach girls to live a *lifestyle* of faith.

Through the captivating, Christ-centered, historical fiction stories of Elsie Dinsmore, Millie Keith, Violet Travilla, and Laylie Colbert, each Club member will come to understand God's love for her, and will learn how to deal with timeless issues all girls face, such as bearing rejection, resisting temptation, overcoming fear, forgiving when it hurts, standing up for what's right, etc. The fun-filled Club meetings include skits and dramas, application-oriented discussion, themed crafts and snacks, fellowship and prayer. What's more, the Club has everything from official membership cards to a Club Motto and original Theme Song!

For more info about our Girls Clubs, call or log on to:
www.alifeoffaith.com • **1-800-840-2641**

Check out
www.alifeoffaith.com

- Get news about Violet, Elsie & Millie
- Find out more about the 19th century world they live in
- Learn to live a life of faith like they do
- Learn how they overcome the difficulties we all face in life
- Find out about *A Life of Faith* products
- Join our girls' club

A Life of Faith® Books
"It's Like Having a Best Friend From Another Time"

What readers are saying...

Nicole, age 17
I really love the Violet stories. They make me feel like I have a very special friend.

Brittanni, age 16
I love the Violet books. I fell in love with Elsie, then with Millie. Now I'm totally in love with Violet.

Heiði, age 15
After reading the Violet books, I felt better about growing up.

LaTel, age 14
The Violet stories have made everything in my life much better! Now I don't think about what I can do for myself but what I can do for others. I'm also a stronger Christian now!

Jorдan, age 13
I love the Violet stories! They inspire me to be a better Christian and to help people who need to be helped. Her stories are really fantastic! When I started reading her books I just could not put them down. They are so interesting!

Tina, age 12
I really like the Violet books because they are focused on Christ, and they are exciting stories. I cannot wait to read the other Violet books as soon as they come out! Thank you so much for your ministry!

Aдbley, age 11
THE VIOLET BOOKS WERE WONDERFUL!!! They have many life lessons in them. I really enjoy reading about someone so young having so much faith and courage. She is an inspiration to us all.